Spirits of San Antonio
and South Texas

Docia Schultz Williams
and Reneta Byrne

Republic of Texas Press
an imprint of
Wordware Publishing, Inc.

Library of Congress Cataloging-in-Publication Data

Williams, Docia Schultz
    Spirits of San Antonio and south Texas / by Docia Schultz Williams.
        p. cm.
    Includes bibliographical references and index.
    ISBN 1-55622-319-6
    1. Ghosts—Texas—San Antonio.   2. Legends—Texas—San Antonio.
    I. Byrne, Reneta.   II. Title.
    GR110.T5B97   1992
    398.25'0976412—dc20   92-31559
                                          CIP

ISBN1-55622-319-6
10 9 8
9210

All inquiries for volume purchases of this book should be addressed to
Wordware Publishing, Inc., at the above address. Telephone inquiries
may be made by calling:

(972) 423-0090

CONTENTS

This book is all about ghosts . . . spirits and specters, both real and legendary, that have been found to exist all over the historic city of San Antonio and in small towns in the surrounding South Texas area.

ACKNOWLEDGEMENTS

Few books have been written without someone's help, someone's encouragement, and someone's good wishes. Many people have graciously shared their stories and experiences with us. Without them, there would have been no book. It would be impossible to name each one individually, but to all we are extremely grateful. There are, however, several individuals who have truly gone "the extra mile" to assist us in our endeavors.

Sam Nesmith, military historian and psychic, spent much time with us in explaining psychic phenomena and sharing his personal experiences in this realm. He gave us many good story leads and cooperated further by visiting several known haunted locales with us. We are very grateful for all of his help.

The librarian at the Daughters of the Republic of Texas Library, Charline Pavliska, as well as the Alamo receptionist, Diana Lindsey, were very helpful in assisting us in our research. Nellie Weincek, librarian for the San Antonio Conservation Society, Marie Berry and Claire Bass, librarians at the Institute of Texan Cultures were all very helpful to us. John Manguso, military historian and curator at the Fort Sam Houston Museum, provided much information and edited our military section. Mr. Ken Alley of the Leon Valley Historical Society was most kind in assisting our research in that area.

A special thank-you must also go to Mr. Clyde Powers, of Seguin, for his information about that city. John Tolleson, local historian and guide, gave us many valuable leads and several good stories. Detective Frank Castillon, Chief Investigator for the Bexar County Medical Examiner and retired homicide detective, San Antonio Police Department, and Barbara Hunt Niemann, retired homicide detective, San Antonio Police Department, shared their valuable time and expertise with us in our work on several stories.

To Olga Castaneda, a big thank-you for her hours of computer coaching as we worked towards our goal.

Thanks also to Bill and Marcie Larsen of the Alamo Street Restaurant, who have helped so much in the staging of the "Spirits of San Antonio" tours, sharing their personal experiences and their wonderful food with the tour groups.

Lastly, to Roy Williams, who offered unlimited encouragement to us and spent endless hours at the computer, helping to organize our material and prepare it for publishing, to him, mere "thanks" is not nearly enough.

INTRODUCTION

We live in a world where the "unknowns" play an important role in the total sum of things. We've been brought up to the thrills and chills of Halloween, Alfred Hitchcock, "The Twilight Zone," UFO's and "Unsolved Mysteries." That there are unexplained things out there beyond the realms of our human comprehension there is little doubt.

Many people have almost died and report near death experiences. Many intelligent, educated people, unlikely to have been influenced by superstition or imagination have seen something, heard something, or felt something, for which there can be no logical explanation except that it was a "supernatural occurrence."

There has to be another dimension out there, where souls of the dead are sometimes suspended, not quite at peace, not quite ready to give up what they had begun during their mortal lives. Thus, these restive spirits return to make themselves known to those who still dwell in the places they once knew. They come to leave a message, to finish a task, to give a warning, or to watch over a once loved location. Some of them are more restless than others. Doubtless they are caught up in frustration that some task was left undone, some wish was not carried out, or some message was not delivered. Or, perhaps, with some, a crime has not been avenged. These spirits sometimes become very persistent, sometimes violent, in their efforts to make themselves known. These restless spirits return again and again to scenes of their earthly travail, where they must roam in restless anguish for all time to come, or until conditions change to their satisfaction. In extreme cases, so that both these restless souls and the mortals that they torment can rest peacefully, a blessing or exorcism may be necessary.

Since ghosts, which are the spirits, or souls, of dead people, can make themselves known in daylight as well as in darkness, their appearances cannot be relegated to any particular time frame. They can be seen as real flesh and blood entities, or as misty, ethereal apparitions, not quite human in form. Sometimes they can only be heard. There will be an unexplained knocking on a door, a footstep in a hallway, a page turning in a book.

We believe that ghosts may have personalities just like the mortals they once were. The strong ones can work up enough energy to be seen. The weaker, more timid types can work up only enough energy to produce a light footstep or a gentle breeze. And generally, all ghostly appearances are fleeting. Perhaps this is because it takes so much energy to produce their appearances . . . who knows for sure?

In researching this book, we have found there is no chronological order to ghostly appearances, either. Hauntings have nothing to do with "old houses" or old anything, for that matter. In this, the twentieth century, buildings, houses, churches, and museums that are brand new can experience visits from spirits which have not been away from this mortal world all that long, as some of these stories will reveal. Our stories begin with the coming of the first Spanish settlers to south Texas and continue right up to the present time.

We have not attempted to delve into the occult or dark side. This book is not about witchcraft, voodoo, or magical spells. It is simply a collection of interesting stories, well researched and documented. Most are known to be true.

There is so much of life, and death, and life after death, that we do not understand. Nor shall we, until we too have crossed over into that unknown dimension. Therein lies the fascination of the spirit world.

Our stories are presented here, sometimes to explain, sometimes to merely entertain. We hope they will prove as interesting to you, the reader, as they did to us, the researchers.

Docia Schultz Williams
Reneta Byrne

GHOSTS
Docia Williams

Ghosts fly high . . . and ghosts fly low . . .
Where they come from, we don't know . . . .
Ghosts take off in roaring flight,
Most often in the dead of night.
They're often felt in spots of cold,
You feel their presence, we've been told.
Some are large, and some are small,
Some, merely shadows on the wall.
Some are friendly, some are bad . . .
Some are playful, others sad.
They're often heard, on creaking floors,
Opening windows, slamming doors!
Wails and moans they sometimes make,
Making us poor mortals quake!
They like all kinds of dreary places,
Houses, churches, and open spaces . . . .
Sometimes they dwell in mist and fog,
They're heard, we're told, in howls of dogs . . . .
Some, balls of fire seen in the night,
All in black, or dressed in white;
Some show a glimpse of shadowy faces,
Then, they're gone. They leave no traces
To ever let us mortals know
Where they come from . . . or where they go . . . .

CHAPTER 1

Public Buildings and Historic Landmarks

Many of San Antonio's haunted landmarks and buildings to which the general public has ready access are included in this chapter.

STRANGE THINGS AT NIGHT
Docia Williams

When the sun comes up and the moon goes down
The spirits seek rest from the sunlit town.
But when once again the day's work ends
They'll come again, these restless friends
To the Governor's Palace, down in the well . . .
Or the John Wood Courthouse, we've heard tell;
At the Alamo the spirits will roam
And at old Ft. Sam they're also "at home."
In the tall watchtower east of town
The ghost light shines when the sun goes down.
At the haunted tracks where the train runs by
The children's spirits are still heard to cry;
In churches, and buildings, and old public places
In parks, and graveyards, and open spaces.
Take heed, my friends, lest you faint from fright
You'd best be at home in the dead of night!

Remember the Alamo

The most famous landmark in San Antonio is, of course, the Alamo. We have found much evidence regarding the spirits of the past which seem to cling to the historic old building. Checks into library and newspaper files and interviews with museum curators and librarians have brought forth many known, and some more recent, stories worth the telling.

First built as a Spanish mission known as Mission San Antonio de Valero, the old chapel and adjacent long barracks building have been the scene of many turbulent happenings over the years. There were Indian uprisings as well as the monumental Battle of the Alamo which was fought on March 6, 1836, at which time all of the valiant Texas defenders were killed by the overwhelming Mexican forces under General Lopez Antonio de Santa Anna.

General Santa Anna had decreed that there would be no mercy given to any of the defenders, and none was asked nor received. In just a few hours of fierce fighting, all the Texas forces were annihilated, their lifeless corpses left lying where they fell. Because there were none of their own number left to bury them, and the remnants of the Mexican army were busy

taking their own dead off for burial, Santa Anna gave the orders to burn the Texan dead.

Old records indicate there were two, possibly three, funeral pyres prepared, and the bodies were stacked "like cordwood" to smolder for days. Denied the dignity of a Christian burial, killed in sudden and violent action, it is no wonder that even today there are many accounts of "strange things . . . noises . . . cold spots" associated with the Alamo and the long barracks museum where the fiercest of the fighting is reported to have taken place.

Although the exact locations of the funeral pyres are unknown, sketchy accounts handed down over the years, largely by word of mouth, indicate that at least one was located on the old "Alameda," a cottonwood-tree-lined avenue located where East Commerce Street is today. Just east of the location of St. Joseph's Catholic Church, there was a boarding house named Ludlow's at what is now 821 East Commerce. There was a peach orchard in back of the boarding house.

Witnesses to the events, both small children at the time, were interviewed by the late Charles Merritt Barnes in an article in the *Express-News* which ran on March 26, 1911. He had interviewed Don Pablo Diaz and Enrique Esparza, who had been around eight years old at the time of the battle. Both vividly recalled the burning funeral pyres and the stench of the smoke which filled the air for days. From these interviews, Barnes concluded the bodies were burned in two pyres, one in the Ludlow yard and the other on the south side of the street some 250 yards east.

We came across another story which concerned the location of the fire station now located east of the Alamo on Houston Street. When it was built in 1937, charred bones were unearthed at that location, which might bear out the possible theory there were three, instead of two, funeral pyres.

By coincidence, when we were browsing in the new Brentanos bookstore on the lower level of River Center Mall, the subject of books dealing with ghosts came up. The young man waiting on me was quick to volunteer the information that "strange things" had been happening in that establishment, and they might possibly have their own resident ghost. He reported that lights would go on and off, books would be moved about, and the cash register would open and close of its own volition. He reported there was a "cold spot" in one corner of the shop. In checking around, it seems the shop is located just about where the Ludlow boarding house would have been, and the peach orchard in back where one of the pyres was reported to have been. He further went on to say that on March 6 of 1991 lights had gone off and on all day, and other unexplainable things had happened. That date is of course the anniversary date of the battle and the subsequent burning of the Texan dead which followed.

Numerous historical accounts have mentioned that after Santa Anna and his forces surrendered to the Texans under General Sam Houston on April 21, 1836, at the Battle of San Jacinto, orders were sent to the small Mexican force remaining in San Antonio to evacuate and retreat south. They were ordered to destroy the Alamo before their departure.

General Andrade, who was in command, gave his subordinate, Colonel Sanchez, the order to send a party of men to blow up the chapel. Several men left for the task but soon returned, saying they could not destroy the building. Their faces showed stark terror, and no amount of persuasion could force them to go back to the building. They reported having seen strange figures which they described as "diablos" (devils) . . . six ghostly forms standing in a semicircle holding swords, not of steel, but of fire, blocking their entry to the building. They were terrified and fearful of the consequences if they should destroy the building, they reported back to their commander. It is said General Andrade went himself to the place and was also confronted by the same figures. And so it was that the building was left intact, as the Mexican army marched out of San Antonio.

Although, periodically, someone reports hearing strange noises, such as voices, marching footsteps, and moans, the last known sighting of anything supernatural took place over a hundred years ago. In 1871 the city of San Antonio decided to dismantle the last remaining part of the original mission (other than the chapel and long barracks, which remain today). This section was the two rooms on either side of the main gate of the south wall. Late one evening, before these were destroyed, guests at the Menger Hotel watched in shocked amazement as spectral forms marched, perhaps in protest of the desecration, along the walls of the rooms.

The *San Antonio Express News* of February 5, 1894, had a most interesting article concerning the Alamo: "The Alamo is again the center of interest to quite a number of curious people who have been attracted by the rumors of the manifestations of alleged ghosts who are said to be holding bivouac around that place so sacred to the memory of Texas' historic dead. There is nothing new about the stories told. There is the same measured tread of the ghostly sentry as he crosses the south side of the roof from east to west; the same tale of buried treasure and the same manifestations of fear by the American citizen of African descent, as he passes and repasses the historic ground. The only variation appears to be in the fact that the sound of the feet on the roof has been heard as late as five o'clock in the morning by the officer in charge, who says that as a matter of fact, however, the sounds are never heard except on rainy, drizzly nights. He attributes the whole matter to some cause growing out of the condition of the roof during rainy weather, but forgot to give any reason why the same causes that produced the sounds at night did not produce like sounds in daylight hours." (Note: in 1894 the city was using the Alamo property as a police headquarters.)

The article continues: "A new feature of the case was presented Saturday night when the spirit occupants of the old building were for the first time brought to bay and made to disgorge the mission of their restless presence in the place. Leon Mareschal, an old and respected citizen living at 1001 San Fernando Street, accompanied by his fourteen-year-old daughter, Mary, called at police headquarters and introduced themselves to Captain Jacob Coy, who was on duty at the time, stating that they could establish communication with the ghosts. Captain Coy gave the parties two chairs and permitted them to use the little jailroom adjoining the station office. Mr. Mareschal placed his daughter in a trance and told Captain Coy to speak to the spirits through the medium. 'Do you see the spirits?' asked Coy. 'Yes, they are men,' came in a faint voice from Miss Mareschal. 'Then get them to form in line and ask them who they are,' continued Capt. Coy.

"The young girl nervously twitched her head from side to side and announced that the ghosts had fallen in line. Immediately thereafter the medium spoke again, saying: 'The forms say that they are the spirits of the defenders of the Alamo.'

"This answered the question in a very general way. It was not satisfactory, but Captain Coy decided not to press the matter until a little later on. 'Now, then,' continued Coy, 'what is the object of their visit and noise in the building at night?'

"After a few seconds the young girl in the trance spoke in a low but firm voice: 'They say that there is buried in the walls of the building $540,000 in $20 gold pieces. They also say that they are anxious to have the money discovered and have been waiting for a chance to communicate with the people on earth about it and have it discovered. They will relinquish all claim to the treasure in favor of the person who finds it.'

"'Now, just where is this treasure buried?' asked Capt. Coy.

"Miss Mareschal fidgeted a little nervously and her words were scarcely audible. 'It's in the wall near that room,' said the medium, pointing towards the dingy little apartment in the southwest corner of the Alamo without looking. 'It's in the wall at that . . .' here Miss Mareschal broke short feebly and rubbed her eyes and the trance was broken.

"It was after midnight, nearly one o'clock in fact, when Leon Mareschal and his mediumistic daughter left the old Alamo. Those who believe in spiritualism lay considerable confidence in the result of Miss Mareschal's interview with the spirits, and it is currently reported that the local Psychical Society will investigate the alleged phenomenon.

"Yesterday all sorts of rumors had gained currency, among them one that the officers in charge of the building were afraid to stay there. This brought a squad of four soldiers from the post who volunteered to hold the fort against the ghostly visitors. Their offer was declined with thanks."

That article was printed nearly a hundred years ago. Strange, but true, those who guard the Alamo now during hours of darkness have told of unexplainable sounds and the feeling of "presences." Is it because the gold is still there, being zealously guarded by spirits until the right finders come along?

Three years later, there appeared still another article about the Alamo in the *Express*, with a new explanation for the hauntings. This article described a visit to the landmark by a number of tourists from out of the state, and ran on August 23, 1897. The article stated: "As a climax to their visit the tourists are told the story of the ghosts of the Alamo and are shown the dark, gloomy recesses in the rear of the building where moans and hissing whispers and the clanking of chains are sometimes heard on wild stormy nights. The disturbing specters are supposed to be those of the errant monks who cried in chains for violating their monastic holiness in the old days when the Alamo was a Franciscan mission. That ghosts haunt the Alamo is claimed to be a well-substantiated fact. The discovery was made only a few years ago by the policemen who were stationed there when the building was used as a sub-police station, and created a great sensation at the time. Some time ago a number of prominent spiritualists held an all night seance there and are said to have had a very interesting and profitable conversation with the specters."

A very recent feature article in the Sunday magazine section of the *Express News* dated January 27, 1991, blared the headlines: "John Wayne's Ghost Remembers the Alamo." Seems the story first ran in the *National Inquirer*! Questions about ghosts at the Alamo museum are usually referred to Charles Long, who was curator of the Alamo museum for fifteen years and currently is the curator emeritus. Long did take Wayne on a tour of the historic mission when the actor was filming the movie *The Alamo* some years back. Wayne's widow, Pilar, wrote in his biography that the story of the Alamo is the epitome of everything he (Wayne) identified with and believed in: toughness, courage, and patriotism . . . so if his spirit comes back to visit the Alamo, it is no doubt to just "visit" with the brave men who defended those ideals and were willing to die for them. (We haven't been able to locate anybody who has heard or seen "The Duke" around, but we thought it a story interesting enough to mention, anyway!)

The *News* article concerning Wayne also mentioned that Joe Holbrook, a widely known San Antonio psychic who counts his ability to communicate with spirits among his special talents, was called upon to visit the Alamo. "He agreed to visit the Alamo to see what sort of ghostly energy he could pick up," the article states. "Holbrook's psychic powers started kicking in even before he reached the shrine," according to the *Express* writer, Craig Phelon. "During his drive downtown he began to pick up images of the Battle of the Alamo.

"In particular, he tuned in on a figure unknown to Alamo history, who he says was one of the real unsung heroes of the Alamo. He was a humble bootmaker named 'Buttons' Morgan. 'Buttons' was obviously a nickname. The psychic said he couldn't pick up Morgan's real first name, but the man apparently was one of the bravest Alamo defenders. He also was devoted to taking care of the wounded soldiers."

Holbrook discussed the nature of spirits with author Phelon. "They don't just linger around the same place all the time," he said. "Anytime you have any place where people have died, you're going to have a spirit sighting from time to time."

Phelon goes on to say, "We enter the shrine and he says ... 'with all these people in here it will be hard to pick up any energy.' But then he is drawn to the room to the left of the main entrance. 'There are six of them right in here,' he says.

"Even though the room appears empty, Holbrook says he can see the spirits. 'The funny part of it is, they're from the other side. They're Santa Anna's men, and they are still in their Mexican army uniforms.' Holbrook stands at the entrance to the room, as if listening ... then offers to supply their names.

"He picks up the name of three of the spirits ... two are brothers, Raul and Pablo Fuentes. They were seventeen and eighteen when they were killed. 'The other one is what we would call a lieutenant. His name is Pedro Escalante,' he says. 'They went over the line and helped these guys. They didn't want this battle. They came over to persuade the defenders to give up and stop fighting. For that they were killed.'

"'The lieutenant spirit gives this information,' says Holbrook. Then he adds, 'You want me to ask about John Wayne?' After a brief silent conference with the spirit, Holbrook brings back the verdict. 'I confirm this is true,' Holbrook quotes the spirit. It seems Wayne's spirit doesn't hang around all the time, but he comes to visit about once a month or so, says the psychic. 'The reason John Wayne comes here, the lieutenant says, is that this place rejuvenates him in some way. To him, the Alamo stands for the freedom of all mankind.'"

Holbrook says. "He considers this the guts of freedom right here. That's his phrase ... that's the way he describes it, according to the lieutenant."

Our theory is, that since the men who died in defense of the Alamo were cremated immediately after the battle, without a proper Christian burial, their spirits are still restive and just keep returning to the site where their lives ended so suddenly and violently.

Chapter 1

The Alamo doesn't seem threatening or frightening to us. It pulls at our heartstrings when we enter. We are filled with reverence and respect when we enter into this shrine to freedom. Under the gentle custodianship of the Daughters of the Republic of Texas, the Alamo has fallen into tender, loving hands. The dignity of those who died defending it is well preserved, and the turbulence of its past now rests in the pages of history. Our fervent hope is that the spirits of those brave defenders have at last found their eternal peace.

The Voice in the Elevator Shaft

The impressive round building on the Hemisfair Plaza grounds that is known today as the John J. Wood Federal Courthouse was built in 1968 to house the United States Pavilion during the World's Fair known as Hemisfair. After the exhibition closed, the lovely building was "recycled" to become a Federal Courthouse. After the tragic assassination of Federal Judge John J. Wood, in May of 1979, the courthouse was named in his honor.

An interview with a former night security guard at the building revealed that the building has "something unusual" there, besides the judges, magistrates, and their staffs. We were told that several years back, as she was acting as a police officer and control operator in the building, she had a very unnerving experience. She was in the ground floor hallway near the back elevator where detainees would be escorted in and out of the building. As she came to the elevator, she distinctly heard a man's voice calling loudly, "Help! Help me! Won't you please get me out of here!" She looked in the elevator

and in the hallway and then down the elevator shaft, but there was no one to be found. She was so positive she had heard the voice that she started avoiding the elevator, using the stairs whenever possible. She did not mention what she had heard to any of the other security staff as she was afraid they would think she had gone a bit "off." Then, one day sometime later, one of the other guards, who has since passed away, asked her if she ever used the back elevator. She told him she really preferred the stairs. The man then went on to mention to her that he had been hearing "a voice in the elevator." She then confessed to him that she had also heard it, and they realized they had heard the same sounds, but at different times. Her associate also said he had heard "other things," too.

Later, when she and another guard were on duty they distinctly heard loud hammering one night coming from the roof area. A careful search revealed nothing there, but after they left the area, the hammering resumed.

Several times, in one of the storage rooms, voices were heard. Windows and doors which had been carefully secured would be found to be unlocked. Doors would sometimes open and close, and lights would go on and off at will, yet the motion sensors would never activate the alarm system.

We also talked with another former security guard. This interview revealed that once when she was making her rounds of the quiet and darkened building late at night, she came into the courtroom which Judge Wood had used. She turned on the lights and was startled to see a man sitting at the judge's bench. He was turned sideways and was in a very relaxed position. A second hard look and he had disappeared! She said other guards also reported having seen the same apparition, and in the same place. Maybe this was the spiritual manifestation of Judge Wood, just watching over the courtroom which he loved and served so well in life.

The Ghost of San Pedro Playhouse

We first learned about a ghostly resident at the San Pedro Playhouse, home of the San Antonio Little Theatre (known locally as "SALT") through reading a brief article in the magazine of the *Express News* in October 1989. The ghost described in that article was that of a stocky man of medium build, balding, and rather elderly. He was said to wear a white shirt with the sleeves rolled up.

The article told the story of how two girls went through the downstairs area, looking for a purse one of them had left in the theatre. They saw the purse, but not before first seeing just a pair of hands and a portion of a white shirt!

Our interest thus aroused, we decided to check with the theatre staff. We were able to talk with Jackie Sparks, long a well-known performer and dance choreographer. Jackie had seen another ghost! She said several years ago she was alone in the old building except for Lorenzo, the custodian, and someone else who was up in the front office. She came up from the downstairs dance rehearsal area to report that the coke machine was empty. She said she came up across the stage area and just happened to look up. There, high above the stage on the grids, about halfway across, was a man in military

fatigues. She thought at first it might be the technical director, but when she called out to him, he did not answer. She said she went on through the theatre and found the custodian and asked him who else was in the building. He went with her back to the stage area immediately. No one was up on the grids! She said there would not have been enough time for whoever it was she saw to have crossed the grid and have gotten down the ladder and down on the stage by the time she returned.

Ms. Sparks said she told some of the other performers about this later, and they told her they had also seen the same man at different times.

At other times, when she would be the last to depart after a rehearsal, Ms. Sparks said she would hear "strange noises" in the theatre, which made her very uneasy. She tried to attribute it to the fact it was just an old building, and old buildings sort of "creak and groan." She also added that when it would be her turn to open up, she didn't like to go into the building alone, and would try to wait for someone else to show up before she entered the empty theatre. She is still actively involved in the theatrical productions, and who knows? The ghost may be just waiting for a chance to perform!

Flushing Water and Boiling Wax

Unexplained "happenings" have occurred from time to time at the West Drexel location of the Bexar County Mental Health and Mental Retardation Group Activity Adult Services Workshop building. Two former night security guards told us what they had experienced. Many times, they said, "flushing noises" would be heard coming from both the ladies' and men's restrooms, in the secured and empty building. A careful check revealed that no one was in either place. The toilets would just flush of their own accord!

One of the ladies told us, when she was on duty very late one night, she was suddenly startled by the sounds of loud band music coming from the warehouse area. She switched on all the lights and discovered a clock radio playing. It was always disconnected at 5 p.m. when the last occupants left the building each day. It had been plugged in at midnight and the music turned up, full volume. She knew it had just been plugged in, because the clock still read 5 p.m.

There is a large room where craft projects are taught. One night, a large cauldron of wax used in candle making was found to be "boiling . . . like it was almost ready to explode," during one of her security rounds. On her previous rounds the burners were turned off and the wax was congealed. There was no one in the tightly secured building at the time. On the same night, she heard boxes tipping over and falling off the shelves, but a thorough search of the building revealed no intruders.

At other times, both guards said when they made their rounds all the doors and windows would be locked. Subsequent rounds would find some of them had been unlocked. One time a very large garage-like door was half open, yet the alarm had not sounded.

Both guards told us that many unexplainable things went on in that building during the years they had worked there. The only "outsider" they ever discovered was just one small rat . . . and even a very large, very healthy rat couldn't have caused that much commotion!

An "Extra" at the Express News

A chance meeting at a club function led to an interesting interview with Helen Lampkin, senior sales executive for the *San Antonio Express News*. A stunning professional woman who looks as if she just stepped from the high fashion section of *Ebony Magazine*, Helen is not the sort of person given to making up ghost stories. But in February of 1990 she went for a smoking break to the designated area on the third floor of the *News* building on Avenue E. The area, which she took me to see, is just a hallway, where there is a stairwell and a freight elevator, outside one of the newsrooms. She said she had just lit a cigarette, when suddenly she felt a warm breath at her right shoulder. She turned her head and saw the figure of a slightly built man in a black jacket . . . "a good, rich, heavy fabric," she said, at her side. Another glance, and he was gone as suddenly as he had appeared. Totally unnerved, she ran into the newsroom and told her friend Dayna Boren what she had seen. She says she knows the man was there, and her only explanation is the figure she saw was a ghost. She still avoids that part of the building.

Lampkin went on to say while this was the only time she had ever had such an experience in the *News* building, it was not her first encounter with the spirit world. She lives with her elderly parents on Martinez Street on the far east side, in a fairly new house in which no one has ever lived except her family. However, from time to time she and her mother have seen two different figures appear. There is a young woman dressed in a beautiful white gown who is frequently seen climbing the stairs. They always see her from the back and have not seen her face. And, in the entry into the dining room, on numerous occasions they have seen a slightly built man, wearing "old fashioned clothing," a sort of derby hat and a rust colored jacket and trousers. His appearances are fleeting, and she says numerous friends and family members have seen him appear and disappear. She believes she may have a certain sensitivity to seeing spirits and that is why she also saw the figure at the *News*.

Jerry Salazar, who works in the national ad section of the paper, also told me of feeling "strange things" on the third floor of the *News* building. He says he sometimes felt dizzy . . . like there was an "electric wave" passing through him. Once he felt someone, or something, blow warm breath on the back of his neck, and he had often heard someone call "Jerry . . . Jerry" in a husky, whispering voice, when he was alone at his desk. He described himself as a "sensor" . . . that is, someone sensitive to certain things. He lives in the downtown area, in an apartment at Martin and Santa Rosa. One night he said he was awakened by a "commotion" outside. He looked out his window and plainly saw a group of Indians around a campfire on the banks of what was San Pedro Creek (now it is walled in, like a canal). There was a little girl with them and she was crying and struggling, as if trying to get away. He said one of the men started rubbing out the fire, scattering the ashes with his moccasin. Thinking maybe he was just dreaming, or at least sleep-walking, Jerry got back into bed. Still disturbed, he got out of bed and made his way back to the window. The Indians were still there. He finally went back to bed. The next morning he went out to the spot and saw what looked like ashes from a campfire. (It is a well-known fact that parties of Indians used to camp along the banks of San Pedro Creek.)

Salazar went on to say that last year, as he was walking along Main Avenue where several buildings had been torn down to widen the street and make a parkway, he saw a woman poking around an area where there were some old bricks. Jerry stopped to chat with her and noted the bricks said "Laredo" on them. This interested him, because he had grown up in Laredo and did not recall a brick company there. The woman told him they were "very, very old bricks." She said it was a shame that a street was going to be there because "there are many valuable things buried here if only someone would dig here." He asked her if money was buried there. She said, "yes, and many other things of value, too." He talked with her a few minutes, then turned and walked away. After he had gone just a few steps, he turned and looked back. The woman had totally disappeared! The area he had seen her was open and there was no place she could have gone that quickly. He believes she might have been the ghostly caretaker of some long hidden valuables, which, unfortunately, are now firmly sealed beneath Main Avenue.

The Professor Who Never Left

Since 1886 the San Antonio Academy has provided an educational background for some of San Antonio's most illustrious citizens, and the prestigious old school is still going strong!

Along with "old schools" come some good "old stories," and we are indebted to Cathy Cummins, the Enrichment Director at the Academy, for this one!

There was a professor named Jim Roe, who began his teaching job at the Academy back in 1922. Previously, he had been employed as a school superintendent in a small rural school near Shreveport, Louisiana.

When Roe arrived to take his new position, Colonel William Bondurant, Senior, the commandant, personally went to the railroad station to meet him. They rode the streetcar back to the school where Professor Roe was to reside for the next fifty years, from 1922 until his death in 1976.

The teacher of English and reading lived a very private and frugal existence. He seldom left the environs of the Academy. He customarily cashed a ten dollar check every Monday and then walked to nearby stores to buy his weekly supplies. Penurious to the extreme, he especially liked to shop at a store where he could buy day old bread at reduced prices! It's said the old prof was adverse to even buying a newspaper. Instead, he preferred to "recycle" papers discarded by other staff members.

Professor Roe evidently had few relatives. He did have a nephew who worked for the railroad in Bakersfield, California. The only vacation he ever took during all the years he spent at the Academy was a trip to see this nephew.

As the years passed by, the old professor began to lose his ability to teach, or to even help the boys in the boarding school department, where he had assisted serving in the dining room. Because he had no other place to go, the administrators allowed him to live upstairs in the Stribling House on the campus. In the mid-1970s he was relieved of all duties. In his senile state, he had begun to serve pancakes with his fingers, and there had been complaints from the students of his lack of delicacy in serving the food.

From then on, Roe, who was eighty-six by then, took to staying in his room most of the time. Only rarely was he seen on the campus, strolling among the roses in the courtyard or picking up pecans in the fall of the year.

Finally the time came when the professor had not been seen for three days. Colonel William Bondurant, Junior, who had become the chief administrator, became concerned and went to check on him. He was shocked to find Professor Roe lying under his bed, dead! Apparently he had tripped over the long string from the waistband of his pajamas, couldn't get them off, and had become entangled and trapped. It was a sad ending to a long and largely solitary life.

Found next to the body under the bed was a locked cash box. The police came and recovered it. The professor had left a will on file with the Percy Company downtown. During his frugal life he had amassed an estate of $264,000!

Cathy Cummins told us that many people think the spirit of the professor is still there, wandering around near his old room upstairs in the Stribling Building. The first time she felt his presence was when she saw a "bright, white light." Sandy Dunn, another staff member, once remarked, "Say, what's with that thing upstairs?" after he had investigated the room. Cathy said she first felt his presence in August about five years ago. She said she was extremely sensitive to that sort of thing, and told us other staff members had also "felt a presence" at the top of the stairs near the professor's old room.

Maybe Professor Roe's spirit is around for a reason. His money was disposed of according to the directions left in his will. However, a cardboard box was found in his room that contained his written works. The manuscript, done more than twenty years ago, contains writing that is as contemporary in context as if it had been just written today.

Cummins thinks the professor is waiting for the Academy to publish his works. It might become a best seller and a continuing legacy to the Academy he loved and served so long!

Jose Navarro's Haunted Homestead

In downtown San Antonio, settled right beside the old Bexar County Jail, there is a quaint old world "compound" of houses, clearly dating from another era. The buildings, which are located on South Laredo at West Nuevo streets, are a low one-story house, a two-story corner building, and a small adobe and limestone three-room building that is barely visible, out back. All are surrounded by a white fence on the Laredo Street side, and a stone wall down the West Nuevo Street side.

These buildings comprise the former homestead of a famous Texas patriot, Jose Antonio Navarro. One of the two native born Texans (the other being his uncle, Francisco Ruiz) to sign the Texas Declaration of Independence, Navarro and his wife, Margarita, purchased the land in 1832. The plot of 1.2 acres lay between the San Pedro Creek and the old road leading to Laredo. The neighborhood in which the property was located was called "Laredito," or "little Laredo," because it was situated on the old highway to the border city.

At the corner of the property there is a two-story limestone building that once served as Mr. Navarro's law office. The

building is very much as it was when originally built, with quoined corners, and consists of two square rooms, one upstairs, and one directly downstairs.

The exact date the Navarros built their house and office is not known. It was certainly built sometime after 1832, as a two-room house with a one-room detached kitchen of adobe brick. The bricks were made of clay-rich soil, lime, and limestone chips and water. Each sundried brick weighed approximately thirty-five pounds. At some point the Navarros enlarged both the house and the kitchen. Workers joined three limestone rooms to the original adobe structure to make an L-shaped five-room structure. Two limestone rooms were also added to the original adobe kitchen.

Mr. Navarro was a member of the ill-fated Santa Fe Expedition in 1841. General Santa Anna sentenced the Texas patriot to life imprisonment in Mexico, but he was able to finally escape. He made his way back to San Antonio in 1845. The Navarros owned a ranch called the "San Geronimo" which was located some forty miles to the east of San Antonio, and they spent most of their time there. They used the town house on their visits to San Antonio. In 1853 they sold the ranch and made their permanent residence in town, where they lived until Jose passed away in 1871.

The Texas Parks and Wildlife Department beautifully maintains the restored complex of house, office, and kitchen. They've even planted a typical "kitchen garden" of the 1800s out back of the adobe kitchen. A pleasant porch shades the back portion of that building. Hollyhocks and roses and other old fashioned plantings border the house and adorn the patio where the old covered well is located between house and kitchen.

Along with all this early South Texas charm, there's the opinion among people who have been closely associated with the house at one time or another that there are a few "spirits" lurking around as well!

David Bowser, author of *Mysterious San Antonio* and resident of San Antonio, says that the house seems to be the main area of psychic disturbances. Footsteps have been heard, "cold spots" felt, furniture has been moved and rearranged, and there's a rocking chair that sometimes gets to rocking when there's no sign of wind or draft! David tells the story about the state employee who was working at the house on a restoration project and decided to sleep there at the house. He slept in the same room where Navarro died on January 13, 1871. Sometime in the middle of the night he suddenly awoke feeling very uneasy. Finally, feeling almost panicky, he arose and walked outside the room onto the porch. He chanced to glance upwards, and there, in one of the upstairs attic dormer windows, was a face staring at him! A careful search turned up nothing . . . at least nothing in human form!

Our friend, Sam Nesmith, who is both a historian and a psychic, visited the place and had a very strange experience. First, when he entered the house, a large cabinet started to teeter and would have fallen over had not a staff member come to assist him in righting the massive piece of furniture. Then, Sam said he went out of the house and crossed over to the kitchen building. There, in a room which he said he believed had been a laundry, he clearly saw the figure of a young man, cowering in a corner. His face was contorted with pain and he seemed to be out of breath. He had been shot in the leg, Sam believed, and was hiding in the room where he finally bled to death. Sam has never forgotten the look of intense anguish and fear that were reflected in the eyes of the youth he saw that day.

In 1834 Jose Antonio's brother Eugenio was the victim of a murder. Shot by what was referred to as a "vindictive assailant," Eugenio was only thirty-four years old at the time of his death. A lady who visited the Navarro house recently told members of the house staff that she had visited the San Fernando Cathedral Cemetery Number One, where she had seen the Navarro name. That is what prompted her to visit the house. They said that as soon as the women entered the house, she screamed, "Oh, my God! He's here!" "She claimed she could see Eugenio Navarro sitting in one of the chairs in the living room," according to the Park Ranger on duty. The Ranger said the woman told him that Navarro was just sitting there, waiting for someone to come and see him. It was very real to the woman, as she had "chill bumps" on both arms!

Other people have sighted various apparitions on the property at different times. There have been reports of a Confederate soldier, a bartender, and a prostitute. The "lady of the night" was apparently murdered in the room up over the main floor room in the old corner office building, no doubt during the time it had served as a bar. Another story tells of a child who supposedly died in a fire on the second floor and whose little ghostly presence has been reported.

A former resident of the house, Mary Garcia, said she once saw an apparition of a woman going up the outside stairs. She and her mother lived in the house for about eight years and they saw the ghost "four or five times" during that period.

David McDonald, the Parks Ranger now in charge of the Navarro property, is quite an authority on the life and times of Jose Antonio Navarro. He speaks of the statesman with such familiarity one almost feels as if they were personal friends. There is one story McDonald told about Mr. Navarro's reported frugal nature. He hated to spend a lot of money, but at least once he did pull out all stops, because the big piano in the front parlor is really magnificent. Hopefully, his wife was a good musician to have convinced Jose to buy such a lovely instrument!

It is very interesting to note that, although numerous ghost stories have surfaced over the years, none of them seem to implicate Jose himself as one of the ghostly visitors. He was apparently well satisfied with the house and grounds, which were comfortable and spacious; he was well respected in the community and had a thriving law practice, so his spirit apparently rests in peace over in the old San Fernando Cemetery Number One. The restive spirits who have made infrequent appearances over the years may have just been "passers-by" for the most part, just stopping off in that inviting little compound of houses as they made their way through town and on down the road to Laredo!

The Gallery Ghost of La Villita

A couple of years ago we read a most intriguing Halloween feature in the Sunday section of the *San Antonio Express News*. People had written in with their own personal ghost stories. The article which interested us the most had won the first prize.

We were able to contact the writer and have her enlarge upon the story as it appeared in the *Express* . . . and so it is that we can share it with you.

Mrs. Rosalie Doss and her husband, Jim, operated a gallery and lapidary shop in the La Villita area for a number of years. The shop was in a part of what had been first a school and then later an apartment building at 504 Villita Street.

The building has evidently changed hands, and purposes, many times. The Dosses first noticed something "strange" going on when the paintings they had so carefully displayed kept moving from one wall to another. At first, Jim thought Rosalie had moved them, and vice versa, but when they questioned one another they learned that neither of them had moved a single painting!

Then one morning Jim called from the workroom in the back of the store, "why was that customer scolding her child?" Rosalie told him she hadn't heard anything, and that no one had been in the shop during the past hour. Jim insisted he had heard a mother scolding a child. He couldn't hear everything that was being said but he distinctly heard a child say he wouldn't ever do it again.

Soon after that incident, Mrs. Doss thought she heard a customer in the gallery. At first she saw no one there. Then, across the room she saw a shadowy figure move back and forth in front of the windows that faced the back courtyard. She was wearing a large bib-fronted apron over her dress and was busily doing something with her hands. Mrs. Doss drew nearer, and the closer she got, the colder she felt. She took a deep breath and then the figure was gone . . . just disappeared in front of her very eyes! She told her husband of this strange and rather unnerving experience, and he just laughed and told her she sure had a vivid imagination.

But then, suddenly, all the pieces of this strange puzzle came together. One day later on that summer, an elderly gentleman came into the gallery. He was a tourist visiting the area. He told the Dosses he had dropped by to see the place where he had lived as a child, and he remarked how much the place had changed. He told them the building housing the shop had once been the home he had lived in when he was a youngster of eight or nine years of age. He said the area near the windows had been in his mother's kitchen where she had a work table and sink. He said his mother had died not long after they left San Antonio. She had really liked the city, except she thought the river, which is very close to the location, was too near for her comfort, and she would scold the boys whenever she caught them swimming in the river. He said they always promised they wouldn't ever do it again . . . but boys will be boys . . . and of course, they did return to the river.

The man looked around the gallery and remarked that his mother would have loved it. He said she always enjoyed rearranging furniture and moving the pictures and portraits around on the walls . . . she was just "always changing things around."

The Dosses looked at one another; they did not tell the gentleman that his mother was still scolding the boys, and still moving things around, and still working by her kitchen sink. From then on, they thought of her as just a busy, friendly ghost, and she became sort of a good luck talisman to them. They said the whole time they occupied the shop, there was never a break-in, although many of the neighboring shops did suffer robberies. Maybe she scared the would-be burglars with a good scolding!

The Dosses no longer have a shop in that location. In its place is a lovely jewelry store named Chamade. It has been so modernized and remodeled that it is difficult to envision its having once been a home. As far as we know, the ghost has not reappeared since the Dosses departed.

Was the Ghost's Kitchen Invaded?

Whenever artist Lynne McClanahan walks by the building now occupied by the River Art Gallery in the La Villita section of downtown San Antonio, she gets a very strange feeling. Her agitation stems from an incident which took place in 1974 when she was a member of the River Art Group.

As part of her duties at the gallery, Lynne opened and closed the building daily. There is one day she recalls very vividly to this day.

She said it was about five o'clock in the afternoon. She stood on the front porch of the gallery, facing in an easterly direction, and in her view was a patio filled with picnic tables. It was such a charming scene, she decided to commit what she saw to canvas.

She sketched the scene and then paused to drink in the view. She added a few final touches to her painting of the courtyard (which now fronts the Monte Wade Fine Arts Building) and suddenly an unexpected sight came into her line of vision. At the far side of her peripheral view, she glimpsed the figure of a woman. Lynne said, "she was stooped, and looked as if she might have been cooking something." Lynne's conjecture was that the patio area might have been the site of a former dwelling, which had a kitchen. It was here that the ghostly figure was working. Lynne felt strange, as if she might be intruding.

"I think the apparition must have drawn me to that particular area on that particularly day, but she didn't plan on my sketching her kitchen!" Although the figure was not entirely clear, Lynne could identify the figure as a female, dressed in white. "I saw her for about sixty seconds, and then the apparition faded." Lynne said after she had sketched what must have been the woman's kitchen, the spirit never seemed to leave her alone.

Lynne recalled a lot of strange things that happened after the chance encounter. The ghost invaded the gallery, often closing it up. Heidi Hardy, who was in charge of the gallery operation at the time, frequently returned after a short absence to find the gallery locked. The spirit also removed paintings from the wall and placed them on the floor.

Even now, when Lynne views the painting she did that day, which now hangs in her mother's home, she is reminded of the strange little lady she saw in the patio, working away in her ghostly kitchen. "I've always thought that painting was kind of special," Lynne told us.

Another Ghost in La Villita

There used to be a resident ghost lady who made the La Villita area in downtown San Antonio her headquarters. She hasn't been seen in a number of years since the area has become such a tourist attraction. At one time back in the 1950s it was a peaceful, tranquil area, the home of a few shops featuring the work of local artists, craftsmen, and weavers. There wasn't a lot of noise and activity back then.

Stories circulated around town from around 1900 to the mid-fifties that there was a lady, clad in the dress of the late 1800s, her hair pulled back in a bun, often seen around the South Presa entrance to La Villita. Sometimes she left that bailiwick and wandered down La Villita Street, to the small shops that were a short distance from the Presa Street entrance. Her visits became regular enough that the craftsmen, glass blowers, and weavers in the shops in that area just accepted her as a part of the community.

Trinity University rented an unoccupied building that once was used as the Warren Hunter Art School. The two-story structure is used today as the Starving Artists Gallery. The old building had not been modernized at the time the university took the building to be used as a storage place for props for the drama department. Several students came to help erect a light pole to bring electricity into the building.

One day while they were hard at work digging a hole in which to place the light pole, one of the students chanced to look up, and there, standing right beside him, was a little lady in strange clothing who had literally appeared out of nowhere! She spoke first to the hole-diggers and complimented the youths on their work. Then she turned away and started up the stairs to an area where other Trinity students were assembling stage props.

Two of the students, recognizing the "other worldly" qualities of the strange visitor, rushed over to Jesse Sanchez' studios in the Florian House across the courtyard from where they were working. Sanchez, who produced epic murals, portraits, and cartoons, dropped everything when told of the ghostly visitor's appearance. He went to the building where the students had seen her, because although he had often heard of her appearances, he had never seen her personally. Sanchez walked around the building, went up the stairs to the second level, and wandered all over the place. He had hoped to see her, but he found nothing out of the ordinary. Sanchez later said he would have liked to engage her in conversation as he felt she was a "friendly ghost."

One artist, Neva Ellas, who owned a shop in the fifties, thought the ghost must have visited her establishment once. Ellas, who created rag dolls and displayed them on open shelves, said on a windless, still day, a doll suddenly flew off an open shelf, barely missing its creator's head. She was sure the ghost wanted to attract attention!

There have been no reports of the ghost being sighted in recent years. No one knows just where she might have gone. Maybe she was an artist who liked to be around her peers. Or maybe she had been a housewife who had kept house in one of the many little houses now used as shops and studios. Maybe she's satisfied that the La Villita area is prospering and is in good hands. It just isn't necessary for her to keep an eye on the place any longer!

The Eerie Railroad Crossing

In far south San Antonio, out past old Mission San Juan, there's a narrow, tree-shaded lane known as Villa Main Road. It runs on until it abruptly ends, then there's a sharp left turn over a railroad crossing, and the road takes on a new name, Shane Road. There's been a story around San Antonio for years and years (in all fairness to the reader, we have to say we couldn't find any real proof in old newspaper files about the incident, but it keeps surfacing so often in news articles, there must be something to the story!) about a terrible accident that happened at the railroad crossing years ago.

The story goes that sometime in the 1940s (some accounts have even said in the '30s) there was a tragic accident that occurred at the crossing, which involved a freight train and a school bus. It seems that on that particular late fall afternoon, which was misty and cold, the old yellow bus was making its last delivery of school children from the consolidated country

school that then served that section of the county. The ten children reported to have been on the bus ranged in ages from kindergartners to teenagers. As the bus started up over the tracks, an uphill pull, it stalled. And just at that moment, a fast-running freight train, going at a rapid rate of speed towards the unguarded crossing, came speeding down the tracks and slammed into the school bus, killing all aboard.

That's how the story goes. And, there's definitely something strange about that particular railroad crossing. A vehicle, be it a truck, bus, or automobile, can stop completely about fifty yards or so from the tracks, be put into neutral gear (the driver must remove his foot from the accelerator), and suddenly it will start rolling towards, and then over, the tracks! And the strange thing about this is, the road makes a slight uphill grade as it approaches the tracks! Some people have reported they put powder or flour on the backs of their vehicles, and they've seen tiny handprints imprinted in the powder after the trip over the tracks. Others have reported that they suddenly put on their brakes as they approached the tracks, and the frustrated spirits broke their windshields!

We don't know if it is spirits or gravity, like a hidden magnetic field of some sort, that causes the unexplainable movement over the tracks, but there's always a car or two at the place, just checking it out for themselves. And around Halloween, well, there's usually something that amounts to a major traffic jam at the otherwise quiet crossing spot!

Near the accident site, there is a pretty subdivision of very nice houses. As a memorial to the dead children, the streets in the area have been given the names of those who reportedly perished in the accident. There's Shane Road, Cindy Sue, Bobbie Allen, Richey Otis, Nancy Carole, and Laura Lee Way. Some residents in this area have reported hearing moans and cries around the tracks in late afternoons, about the time the tragedy occurred.

One of the strangest stories concerning the event was printed in the *San Antonio Express News* Magazine section on November 26, 1989. Mr. David A. Burnett wrote of a most unusual experience he had as he came home from work on the night of February 13, 1981: "As I was driving along, I noticed a young girl who couldn't have been any older than fifteen, at the edge of old Mission Road. It was cold, and I'd always thought the area was kind of spooky, so I asked her if she needed a ride home. She said yes. She told me her name was Cindy Sue and that she lived off Villa Main Road.

"I wondered what a girl her age was doing out so late. She was quiet to the point of giving me the creeps. She said nothing as we drove along, but I could see through the corner of my eye she was looking at me.

"We approached some old railroad tracks. As we went across, Cindy Sue started squirming in her seat. I asked her what was wrong. She said, 'nothing.' As we arrived at her house, she remained in the car. I quickly assumed she was having problems at home, so I told her I would talk to her parents.

"I rang the doorbell and an elderly man and woman answered the door. I expected her parents to be much younger.

"They both looked at me as if I was crazy when I said Cindy Sue was in my car. The elderly man became upset and told me to get off his property or he would call the police. As I walked back to the car he yelled, 'Quit doing this to us. Let Cindy Sue rest in peace.'

"When I got back to the car, Cindy Sue was gone. I never heard the car door open or shut, she just vanished. I remember that when she got into the car, she locked the door and fastened her seat belt. To my disbelief, the door was still locked and the seat belt still fastened. Then I remembered why I'd thought the area was unsettling. Several years ago, a bus accident in the area had killed several children. As a memorial to the children, the street names in the neighborhood had been changed to those of the students who had died in the bus accident. As I drove out of the neighborhood, I noticed the name of the street right before the old railroad tracks, Cindy Sue."

We have to agree with Mr. Burnett. There's something very strange, and eerie, and sad, about the area. We've been out there many times, but we are always glad to drive away and leave the tracks to the little spirits who seem to guard them, trying, apparently, to protect others from a similar fate.

A Voice Cries From the Well

It's called the Spanish Governor's Palace, but actually, the sturdy old stuccoed-stone structure that faces onto Plaza Del Armas (Military Plaza) was constructed to be the "Commandancia," or home of the Spanish Military Commander of the old Presidio of San Antonio de Bejar. It enjoys the enviable reputation of being one of America's finest examples of Spanish Colonial residential architecture, and what's more, unlike other Governor's Palaces scattered over the Southwest, which now serve a variety of purposes such as museums, restaurants, and shops, San Antonio's "Palace" is furnished with authentic antiques of the Colonial Spanish period and looks like a home would have looked in those days. Still easily visible over the entry doors is an "escudo," or coat of arms, bearing the old Hapsburg crest of the Double Eagle, a simplified version of the coat of arms of King Ferdinand VI of Spain. It bears the inscription, weathered, but still legible, "ano 1749, se acabo" (finished in the year 1749). The doors are of hand-carved walnut, copied from etchings of the original doors at the time of the restoration of the building which began in 1928.

There's an aristocratic air about the old building, and one can imagine how the "palace" nickname became attached to the building, since it was probably the most palatial building in San Antonio at the time of its construction! What grand fetes and parties and banquets it must have hosted, and what interesting and important guests must have enjoyed the hospitality of its candle-lit chambers!

The brochure given to visitors to the Governor's Palace offers the following historical information: "The Commandancia, originally intended to serve as the residence of the presidio commander, came to represent the seat of Texas government when in 1772 Villa de San Fernando (San Antonio) was made the capital of the Spanish Province of Texas. Then, in later years, after 1822 (Mexico having won her independence from Spain in that year) the Spanish Governor's Palace served as a secondhand clothing store, a tailor's shop, a barroom, a restaurant, and a schoolhouse. In 1928 the building was purchased from the descendants of Jose Ignacio Perez of Spain for $55,000. (Perez had paid 800 pesos for the building in 1804.)

Only after thoroughly researching the original design and materials used in the building was restoration undertaken and completed at the cost of $29,514.61. Authorities state that the Governor's Palace is authentic to the last degree in room arrangement, fireplaces, the thick walls, and brick ovens. Furnishings of the palace include antique pieces from the early 1700s.

One real treasure, and of special interest to Texans, is the beautiful hand-carved secretary desk in the front bedchamber. It was the property of the famous frontiersman and Texas patriot James Bowie!

The Governor's Palace was dedicated in 1931 and since then has been under the capable supervision of the Department of Parks and Recreation of the City of San Antonio.

Today the "Palace" is one of San Antonio's most visited landmarks. Behind the main building there is a lovely shady patio, with a lily pond, a grapevine covered loggia, and a well. At one time this area was probably more utilitarian, as they must have stabled their horses nearby, and perhaps had a kitchen garden in the area, also. Now the restored patio is an integral part of the palace compound. The well, once used for drinking water, is no longer used for that purpose. Tourists toss coins into its depths, believing it to be a wishing well.

And therein lies a story, as told to us by present custodian, Jessie Rico. Rico says he was told in early days there was a robbery and murder that took place at the palace. Since it's a "word of mouth" sort of story, no one knows exactly when it all took place. But be it fact or fiction, this is what Jessie told us. It seems there were no banks in those days to safeguard family valuables. Once, when the family who lived there was away, they left the place in the care of a young servant girl. She was supposed to take care of the house and look after the gold, silver, and other valuables in the palace.

Chapter 1

Robbers were said to have broken in, robbed her of the household treasures, and then bound her and threw her into the thirty-seven-foot well behind the house. She drowned, of course, and was not found until one of the robbers, unable to live with his terrible secret, told what had happened to her.

Rico says it is weird, but at night when he closes up the house and patio, he has often heard strange "gurgling" noises down in the well. Sometimes when he has to go down into the well to retrieve the coins tossed by the tourists he experiences "very strange feelings." Now, Jessie is a big man, and certainly doesn't look as if he'd scare very easily . . . but he definitely doesn't like to be around that well!

We were also told that in the front room to the right of the entryway in the private chapel of the house, there was discovered, during the 1930 restoration, bones buried in the wall behind the small altar niche. They are believed to be the bones of a very small infant. Who it was . . . or why it was placed in the chapel walls, no one knows. It might be speculated that the infant was a stillborn who died in the house. Did weather prevent the little remains from being taken to a cemetery, or did they fear the Indians who often attacked the settlers as they made their way to the cemetery over where the Santa Rosa Hospital is today? Or was there some dark secret buried with those little remains? The spot in the wall, behind a lovely old statue of a Seventeenth Century Virgin is plainly evident, and the mystery still goes unsolved.

Jessie says he has had several strange experiences in the house, just little unexplained noises and feelings of cold spots in certain areas. Sometimes he feels he is being watched. As he closes up at night and turns off the lights in the ancient building, he says he just wants to close up fast and get out . . . and he never looks behind him!

The Old "Spanish Tower"

Going north on Nacogdoches Road, just before you reach Loop 1604, there's a steep hilltop over to the left, with a wooded area surrounding it. A close look will reveal an old stone tower, standing alone on the hill. It has a crenelated roofline, making it look quite Spanish in appearance.

From time to time, reports of "ghost lights" up in the old tower seem to surface. There was an article in a *San Antonio Monthly Magazine* in October of 1981 that suggested the tower might have served as an "outpost for the Alamo." People living in the area are said to have seen what appears to be "ghost lanterns" up there at night sometimes, and since it is on private property, up on a high and fairly inaccessible hill, it would rather rule out the possibility of the lights being from campfires, transients, or teenagers out on a "lark" in the darkness.

Although the magazine article offered the opinion that the light could be from spirits of Spanish soldiers ambushed and overrun by the Indians, we learned from a spokesman for the Historical Society that the tower is not from the Spanish period at all, although the architecture shows a definite Spanish influence. It was built by the man who owned the land back in the 1920s, a retired military officer who had served in Europe during World War I. Much impressed by castles, he built the tower as the first portion of what was to be a castle-like dwelling high on the hilltop. We could not find out why the project was never completed. Perhaps the builder, frustrated because his castle was never finished, is the carrier of the ghostly lantern!

A Museum That Has Both History and Mystery!

It is generally believed by most people that a building has to be very old to be haunted. Not so! Now, granted, a new building may not have as many manifestations as an older property, because more things have happened in older buildings to generate the return of spirits. But there's absolutely no chronological table in which one might categorize ghosts. One building in San Antonio which is of modern construction is the Institute of Texan Cultures, which dates from 1968. The building, which looks a bit like a flying saucer, rests at the foot of the great Tower of the Americas and occupies the land at the corner of Durango and Bowie streets. Owned by the University of Texas, the multipurpose museum, which is equipped with classrooms, changing exhibits, teaching docents, and a fine museum shop, is devoted to the preservation and presentation of the history of the many ethnic cultures which have made Texas the great state we know today. It is equally enjoyed by student groups, tourists, and interested local citizens. Dedicated docents offer history lessons that make each exhibit literally come alive to the visitor.

The first director of the Institute was a dedicated and intellectual historian, a gentleman named Henderson Shuffler. His office was on the upper level of the building. The late Mr. Shuffler smoked a pipe, and according to a former researcher at the Institute, Sam Nesmith, Mr. Shuffler may still come around. Nesmith said he used to come to work on Sunday mornings when he could work alone in the building and get more done. During those mornings, he would often smell pipe smoke wafting from Shuffler's old office. No one else on the staff smoked a pipe!

Then there are the stories concerning the appearance of a man in an orange work shirt, who is seen from time to time. He was a workman, employed during the time the building was under construction. He is said to have committed suicide. The fact he still comes back may just indicate he wishes he had not acted so hastily.

William Ward, Support Service Supervisor, says he knows of a ghost that has been around for at least twenty years. His footsteps are often heard walking down the ramp in the audio-visual room, making a sort of "crunch, crunch" sound. The steps are so often heard that workers in the department have given the spirit a name. They call him "Old John." Old John has been seen or heard in other parts of the building also. The library seems to be a favorite spot of his. He often rearranges books, much to the chagrin of the librarians. He has also appeared in the lower level exhibit areas, and some of the night security guards dislike working there at night unless the areas are completely lighted.

We were told that in the 1970s a worker named Roberto was startled by feeling a "presence" of someone watching him as he cleaned some exhibit cases. The feeling was so strong and unnerving that Roberto asked to be relieved of duty in that part of the building.

We hear that there's often "activity" of an unexplained nature that seems to center around the old 1898 glass-windowed hearse that is part of the French exhibit. It was used in the little Alsatian community of Castroville, just west of San Antonio, from 1898 to around 1930. Guards have reported the door at the back being open. They will close and secure it . . . make their usual rounds, and return to find the door once again is open. This has apparently happened numerous times.

Maybe the spirit of someone carried on their last journey in that conveyance is just trying to get out!

One of the most amazing and puzzling occurrences connected with the Institute took place just this year, in April (1992). The Friday during Fiesta week, a grounds maintenance man named Gerald had a heart attack and died. He had been ill for some time, but his sudden death came as a shock to the staff at the Institute. Gerald was a mildly retarded man, and he loved to work at the place and pass the time of day with the people who worked there.

On Saturday morning, one of the professional staff members, Vivis Lemmons, came to work as usual. As she came up to the back entrance where the staff enters, she saw Gerald come out of the door onto the porch. She spoke to him and he returned just a "hullo" as was his usual custom. She said she did not know him very well, so she did not stop to chat. She did notice that he was very dressed up. He was wearing a tan suit and a very pretty bright blue necktie. She had always seen him before in the dark green uniform worn by the groundskeepers.

Lemmons went into her office. As she was putting her things away and getting her desk in order, she overheard the name "Gerald" mentioned by some of the staff who were already in the room. She said she turned around and said, "Did you mention Gerald? I just saw him outside . . . he surely was dressed up." There was a stunned silence for a moment, and then the others told her that she couldn't have seen Gerald . . . he had died the day before and his funeral was to be that very day (Saturday). She insisted she had seen him, and later she went back to the door where she had seen him and asked the guard who had let her in if he had seen her talking to anyone outside the door. He told her no, but he thought he saw her talking to herself as she walked in!

Lemmons said she learned later that day that a man who worked in the upper level of the museum in what is known as the "Dome area" had also seen Gerald. He had seen the man as he came out of the lower level snack bar, counting his change as he came out. He had not spoken to Gerald, but did plainly recall seeing him. He too noted that Gerald had worn a tan suit and bright blue tie, and thought it certainly was different from his usual work attire.

Staff members who attended the funeral service reported back to Lemmons that the clothing she had described was the attire in which Gerald was clothed for his burial. Mrs. Lemmons believes that the Institute was very special to Gerald . . . and the staff was almost like a family to him. He had just wanted to make one more trip there to make some final goodbyes, and maybe just show them how nice he looked "all dressed up." While everyone could not see him, Lemmons felt privileged that at least she, and one other, saw him that one last time. She feels that some people are more tuned in to psychic phenomena than others and that is how she saw Gerald. She went on to say that the Institute is so filled with artifacts, from ancient to modern, possessions that figured importantly in many lives, that there's just bound to be more "energy" turned loose there than in most places. We are prone to agree with her judgement!

He Can't Leave the Dienger Building

The first time I ever paid a visit to the Dienger Building was in 1970. I had Sunday lunch there with friends in Boerne. The place was then known as the Antlers Restaurant, and I was impressed by both the good food and the collection of hunting trophies that adorned the walls. I never dreamed that one day I might be writing a story about that old building for a book about ghosts!

Today the interesting old building houses the new public library. It is still often referred to, especially by old-timers, as the "Dienger Building" because Joseph Dienger, a leading citizen of the community, and his wife, Ida, had it constructed of cut limestone back in 1884. The Diengers lived in the upper level while maintaining their successful mercantile business, the Dienger General Merchandise Store, on the ground level. It was the first building in Boerne to combine a business and residence under one roof.

The store had offered a wide variety of groceries, arranged in bins and shelves on the ground floor, while the dark cellar beneath cooled meats and wines. The upstairs living quarters also served as a place for community meetings and gatherings

as well. Mr. and Mrs. Dienger apparently loved to entertain, but both were teetotalers. Drinking was something of which neither approved.

Mr. Dienger lived a long, full life, finally succumbing at the age of ninety, peacefully passing away in his upstairs bedroom.

After his death, brothers Charley and Lewelyn Dienger owned the building for a time. Then, later on, Mr. O. M. Scholtz operated a grocery store there. Finally, in 1969 Bob Pegram bought the place and after quite a bit of restoration, converted it into a fine restaurant that operated, under a number of owners, until 1978.

Now old Mr. Dienger had been quite an outdoorsman. He loved to hunt deer in the Texas hill country, and had amassed a large collection of mounted trophy heads. There was also quite a store of deer antlers in the basement, so many, that Mr. Pegram had a lot of them hauled off. This collection gave Pegram the inspiration to name the place the Antlers. The former bedroom of Mr. Dienger was made into an upstairs club with a bar, and was known as the Trophy Room. Here many of the prize trophies were displayed.

Now, it was generally known Mr. Dienger had disapproved of drinking. His spirit soon began to demonstrate this apparent disapproval by slamming doors, rattling windows, and turning lights on and off in the old cellar. Once, Mrs. Dienger apparently helped in the protest, because the silhouette of a woman crossing the Trophy Room was seen. Incredibly, it just passed through a solid wall!

There were enough ghostly shenanigans going on, that Mr. Pegram wanted to keep on the good side of the spirits. He exhibited great courtesy towards the former owners, and wanted to gain their respect as well. For that reason, he began the custom, which would be continued by subsequent owners of the Antlers, of maintaining a table set for the Diengers at the entrance to their former bedroom. There were always immaculate linens, a silver setting, and thin stemmed crystal goblets filled with Mr. Dienger's favorite beverage, clear, pure water! A later owner of the business, Judy Wasson, said that "no one could touch that table. If they left things on it, we'd find them tossed on the floor. Sometimes the water glass would be half empty."

Mrs. Wasson, who now owns another business in Boerne, known as The Closet, told of many events that happened to convince her there really was a resident spirit at the Antlers. She never saw Mr. Dienger, but she often felt his presence. He did not frighten her, however, and she said she actually felt safe when alone in the building because she felt Mr. Dienger would "take care of things." She said she never had anything, not even an ashtray or salt and pepper shaker, stolen during the time she had the business.

One time, Wasson said, one of the ladies who worked there reported a painting, a rather large work, was missing from its usual place in the downstairs ladies powder room. It would have been difficult to get out of the building without being seen with such a large picture. When she entered the building via the kitchen door the next morning, she was surprised to see the picture leaning against the kitchen door. She said a search the night before had not turned the picture up anywhere in the building, so it must have been returned between two a.m. and seven a.m.

Wasson said she made a habit of saying "hello" and "good-bye" to Mr. Dienger, and showing "proper courtesy." She often heard him banging on doors and sometimes he would lock, then unlock them. He frequently locked the outside stairway door to the bar and lounge, just a way of making his dislike of liquor being served there known.

Once when there was a party at the Antlers, Wasson said a man named Jerry Bailey, who was a local automobile dealer, came out of the restroom in a hurry. Someone had tapped him on the shoulder . . . and he had turned to face Mr. Dienger, who was just registering his disapproval of the party!

According to an article in the September 24, 1981, *San Antonio Express News* written by Ed Syers, at least one staff member did see a figure believed to have been Mr. Dienger. Doris Rankin was managing the place, and she recalled one autumn night when she first came across the ghostly presence of Mr. Dienger. One evening the Rankins were getting ready to close . . . it was late. They heard footsteps coming up the stairs in the enclosed stairwell leading to the second floor. A man emerged from the stairwell and at its head, passed their table. Close enough to touch, he was short and compact in an old-fashioned suit and carrying a briefcase. He crossed the lounge and entered the Trophy Room, and then literally vanished.

According to the *News* article, Dienger would even "help out" when the restaurant staff got busy. One lady said her husband had gone to the salad bar. She got back to their table first, and someone pulled her chair out for her . . . only her husband was still poking around the salad bar, and no one else was around! Mrs. Wasson was quick to tell the lady it was just Mr. Dienger, who "helps out when we are busy." She explained he was very courteous about helping, except when they served drinks. With determination, Dienger seemed to resist the lounge's Sunday openings. Almost on the hour, Wasson would find the entry door locked. She would unlock it and then return shortly to find it locked again. She scolded Mr. Dienger and told him to "be good," that she had a business to run!

Mrs. Olive White, who once managed the Antlers, told me many things had happened over the time she was in the building that were difficult to explain. She was, like Judy Wasson, not afraid but she knew the spirits were there. She often heard laughing and talking coming from the upstairs area. It sounded as if a party was going on with "jovial, happy sounds." Sometimes she said she heard the ringing of a telephone, a sort of "muffled ringing" in an area where no telephone was located. When she went down into the basement she often heard footsteps following her, but a turn-around to look revealed no one was there.

Mrs. White said the kitchen help had their stories too. Sometimes there would be a voice saying "kitchen . . . kitchen," over the intercom which connected the private club upstairs with the downstairs kitchen. This would always happen when no one was upstairs!

Mrs. White's son-in-law sometimes worked as a bartender. One time he was startled to have a flashlight hurled at him. And, once, Mrs. White was sitting on a barstool talking to the bartender, when she looked around and saw a young woman, with her back to the room, standing next to the entrance to the men's room. She was looking out where a window had once overlooked the park area below. The figure wore an old-fashioned eyelet cotton petticoat and she had long flowing hair. She finally turned and walked over to the entrance to the ladies' room, which had been the old bathroom in the Dienger's living quarters. After she entered the room, Mrs. White got up and followed her. "No one was there . . . just as I expected." The ghost was not transparent. Mrs. White said, "she looked just like a normal young woman."

As long as the Antlers Restaurant and club operated, the stories of Mr. Dienger and "other visitors" continued to flourish. Then, in 1979 the First National Bank of Boerne took an option on the building and things sort of settled down a bit. However, the bank's director of business development, now Kendall County Judge Garland Perry, said that Mr. Dienger still rattled windows and turned on the cellar lights. And once, when there was a costume party there in the building, in November of 1979, a group of four pretty ladies were asked to pose for a photograph. When the picture was developed, an opaque figure appeared in front of the girls. No one doubts it was Mr. Dienger!

In June of 1991 the fine old building took on still another "career field." It is now the pride of the city of Boerne . . . the new public library! That should really make the spirit of Joseph Dienger happy. There's not a sign of a bar among the book stacks!

CHAPTER 2

Mysterious Hotels, Inns, and Restaurants

HAUNTED HALLWAYS
Docia Williams

Hotels, like houses, can haunted be . . .
By ghosts one can both hear and see.
In inns and charming dining places
Spirits dwell in the hidden spaces.
At one, there's a wraith that walks the hall
And one, there's banging on the wall.
In one, a shadow, dark and scary
Enough to make a traveler wary!
Candles move, and lights go out,
When 'ere the spirits are about.
So when you stop to spend the night,
Perhaps you'd best leave on the light!

Glories and Ghosts at the Gunter

From almost the very beginning of the Republic of Texas, there has been a hostelry at the corner of Houston and St. Mary's streets. In 1837, just one year after the Battle of the Alamo, the Frontier Inn opened its doors to the waves of new arrivals surging into Texas from the East. In that same year, Bexar County was created by an Act of Congress of the Republic of Texas, and John W. Smith was elected mayor. Mayor Smith, known as "El Colorado" because of his red hair, was a hero of the Texas Revolution and the last messenger sent out

from the Alamo by Travis. His wife was the former Maria de Jesus Curbelo, whose family arrived with the Canary Island settlers in 1731.

The Frontier Inn had the best location in the center of the bustling little town that sprawled along the banks of the San Antonio River. Travelers and cattlemen could hobble their horses in clear sight of the stream and cool off in its waters.

The little inn stayed open through two invasions by Mexican armies in 1842. First General Rafael Vasquez hoisted the Mexican flag over the city and the general declared Mexican laws would be in force. After occupying the town for two days, the army moved on without firing a shot. A second invasion was led by a French soldier in the employ of the Mexican forces, General Adrian Woll. In the fall of 1842 he brought a force of one thousand men to retake San Antonio and the Republic of Texas. Two hundred Texans met General Woll's forces at the Battle of Salado Creek north of San Antonio. The Mexicans lost sixty men, while the Texans lost only one in battle, but over fifty were captured and marched to Vera Cruz, Mexico, where they were interned in the infamous Perote Prison. Some Texans escaped and others were finally released and returned to San Antonio.

For over twelve years the Frontier Inn saw many changes in the Republic of Texas from its vantage point on "El Paso" at "El Rincon" (now Houston and St. Mary's streets).

In 1845 Texas became a state of the Union. U.S. troops were dispatched to serve in San Antonio. When the army arrived, there were no government headquarters, storehouses, or living quarters. The Alamo was repaired sufficiently to serve as a quartermaster depot.

In 1846 a man named William Vance, an Irishman from New York, was appointed commissary agent for the United States and came to San Antonio. Soon after his arrival, his brothers, who had operated successful mercantile businesses in both Arkansas and Louisiana, followed him and opened a general store on Alamo Plaza. At the request of General Percival Smith, the brothers Vance agreed to erect a building the army could lease. They negotiated to purchase the old Frontier Inn for $500, choosing it because of its good location. It was soon replaced with a two-story structure facing on Houston Street. In the rear of the building, on St. Mary's at Travis, a barracks was built around a quadrangle, the first army quadrangle in San Antonio. Among officers stationed here were Col. Albert Sidney Johnston and Lt. Col. Robert E. Lee.

In 1861 the Union forces moved out with the famous Fighting Fifth Cavalry, which had been billeted there. The Confederate forces then used the Vance building as their headquarters. At the end of the war, Major General David S. Stanley of the United States Army arrived to take command. Larger quarters than those at the Vance were necessary, and officers were quartered in the French building, while enlisted troops were stationed at San Pedro Springs.

The Vance brothers took back their buildings and they established their business as the Vance House. In 1882 Stephen Gould wrote in his Alamo City Guide: "We have another strictly first-class hotel, and very favorably located, handy for those who come here for business or for pleasure; quiet and cool, yet central; near all the churches, it combines all the elements needed in a hotel home. The proprietor, Mr. E. C. Everett, has made this hotel his hobby, and guests can rely on receiving first-class accommodations at reduced prices. The table has the reputation of being one of the best provided and served in Western Texas." The Guide continued: "Terms are $2. per day. Reduced rates by the week or by the month. Guests arriving by trains at either depot can take the horse cars and be carried to this hotel for five cents."

In 1882 a gentleman from Germany arrived on the scene. His name was Ludwig Mahncke. He was a friend of Kaiser Wilhelm I, and with him be brought customs of his "fatherland." He soon opened a family saloon-restaurant which was characteristic of many European coffeehouses, a place where people could gather and exchange news, make business deals, enjoy refreshments and the camaraderie of others. Mr. Mahncke took an interest in politics and civic recreational needs. He served as an alderman-at-large for two terms, and was a moving force behind the city's establishment of parks. He is still honored by having had Mahncke Park, off Broadway, named in his honor.

Shortly after Mahncke opened the saloon and restaurant, he decided to venture into the hotel business. He took a partner, Lesher A. Trexler, already a successful hotelier, and together they took over the Vance House, adding innovative new conveniences, and renamed it the Mahncke Hotel. It soon became one of the city's leading hotels and a favorite meeting place for cattlemen and businessmen to gather. In the late 1880s the Mahncke, which was an anchor for Houston Street, advertised that it had "no superior in the State." It stated that its rooms were "airy, comfortable, and cleanly." It had all the modern conveniences. Its table was said to be beautifully supplied with everything in season and everything first class. Its rates were reasonable, and last, but by no means least, the managers, Dr. Trexler and Mr. Mahncke, were said to be "especially attentive to its guests."

By the turn of the century San Antonio had become a metropolitan city. Tourism was a big business, and the Mahncke site was central to the city's business section. At this time a group of civic leaders banded together to organize the San Antonio Hotel Company. They decided to buy the corner occupied by the Mahncke and build the most modern hotel in the country, "a palatial structure that would meet the demands of the state's most progressive city." Real estate developer L. J. Hart, along with twelve other local investors, including Jot Gunter, purchased the site from Mrs. Mary E. Vance Winslow in 1907 at a cost of $190,000. Mr. Gunter died before the hotel was completed, but the hotel was named to honor him, as he had been a major financial backer of the project.

The new hotel officially opened on November 20, 1909. It was an eight-story, 301-room structure of buff brick, steel, and concrete, the largest building at the time in San Antonio. It ushered in an era of grand social life in the city. The November 21, 1909 edition of the *San Antonio Light* gave a glowing write-up of the formal banquet that heralded the opening. It was a grand affair, with covers laid for 382 guests . . . the grand ballroom was decorated with roses, carnations, smilax, and greenery. Gigantic horseshoes of flowers signified good luck and prosperity to the new hotel as elegantly attired women and gentlemen in formal dress attended the gala affair. The designer of this grandest of hotels was J. Russell of the St. Louis firm of Moran, Russell, and Gorden, the same firm that had also designed the Hotel Adolphus in Dallas, the Galvez in Galveston, and later, in 1912, the Empire Theatre in San Antonio.

The new hotel became the center for cattlemen to gather. (There was a separate reception room for women, with a private entryway!) It had its own laundry, heating plant, barber shop, and water system with an artesian well in the basement.

In 1917 a ninth story was added, and then, in 1926, three more stories were added, with the "Gunter Roof," which boasted a Japanese garden, as the final icing on the cake. It became a popular place for dining and dancing under the stars. During two world wars the Gunter became "home" to both the Army and Air Force personnel stationed here, continuing its importance as the "Center of Everything."

The Gunter was a home away from home to many famous personages over the years. General John "Black Jack" Pershing, feted for his service on the Mexican border with a banquet at the Gunter, was presented with a blooded horse in the lobby. Western film star Tom Mix also was photographed registering at the lobby reception desk astride his favorite horse, Tony. Will Rogers dispensed his homespun humor there; Max Baer and his brother Buddy spent their free time there while stationed at Lackland Air Force Base; John Wayne called it home during the filming of *The Alamo*. While Harry S. Truman was President, he stayed in the 12th floor Presidential Suite, right across the hall from Speaker of the House Sam Rayburn. Mae West, B. C. Forbes of *Forbes Magazine*, and Gene Tunney were other famous guests of the hotel.

In 1979 Josef Seiterle, representing a Swiss investment group, bought the Gunter and spent over $20,000,000 in completely refurbishing the hotel, restoring it to its past glory. In the spring of 1985 a new porte cochere entrance from St. Mary's Street, topped with a swimming pool, landscaped deck, and exercise room, and flanked by a parking garage, completed the costly restoration. In July 1989 the Gunter joined the huge global network of Sheraton Hotels. It is now part of the "family" of over 500 properties that Sheraton operates in 64 countries. It is the fourth of the Sheraton Corporation's historic hotels, and continues to be the "Place to Meet in San Antonio."

Along with all the pomp and ceremony, and all the business deals that have been culminated in its many years of service, a little intrigue and mystery have crept into the archives of the old hotel as well. Probably the most unusual, fascinating, bizarre unsolved crime in San Antonio police files occurred at the Gunter.

On February 6, 1965, a blonde man in his late 30s checked into room 636 at the Gunter. He registered as "Albert Knox" of Youngstown, Ohio. Later, police found the address he gave was a vacant lot, and the only Albert Knox in Youngstown was a black man who had never visited San Antonio.

During the next three days the man, who was about five feet nine inches tall and weighed around 160 pounds, occupied the room. He was seen going in and out of the hotel several times, accompanied by a tall blonde woman in her thirties.

On the morning of Monday, February 8, the maid on duty, Maria Luisa Leja, said she changed the linen in the room and straightened it up. On the same day, the afternoon maid, Mrs. Maria Luisa Guerra, prepared to check the room. Thinking the occupants had forgotten to remove a "Do Not Disturb" sign on the door, she opened the door with her passkey. As she stepped inside, she saw an Anglo man standing beside a blood-soaked bed. According to an account in the *San Antonio Express News* on February 10, the maid, upon discovering the man, screamed. The man laid a finger against his lips as if cautioning her to be quiet. Then, he scooped up a blood-soaked bundle and disappeared out the door.

Searching the room for clues, the police found what they said were the small footprints of the apparent victim. They also found several cigar butts, one of which bore the imprint of lipstick!

A police dog was brought in to follow the suspect's apparent trail. It led to a window leading to a fire escape. There police found two drops of blood, but the trail turned cold, apparently washed away by a light rain.

In the room they found a suitcase containing a man's shirts, some cheese, sardines, and several empty wine bottles. Officers also found blonde hairs in the room, as well as nylon hose and women's underclothing.

On the bed, officers found the shell of a fired .22 caliber bullet. A .22 caliber slug was found embedded in a wall near a bloodied chair. This led detectives to believe the woman had been shot, possibly with an automatic pistol, from the bed, as she sat in the nearby chair. Bloody trails indicated the slayer had to make several trips to the bathroom, presumably to wash the parts of a dissected body. A recent interview we had with former Detective Frank Castillon, who was a Homicide detective assigned to the case, revealed that during the investigation, a bloody "water line" was found in the bathtub. Detective Castillon's theory is this is where the body was butchered and washed.

Mrs. Guerra, the maid who discovered the man in the room, said the bloody bundle she saw was about a foot high and some 20 inches or so long and wide. Officers said the body of a small boned woman, dissected and blood-drained, could have fit the dimensions of the bundle.

The room was a bloody mess. The mattress and floor were covered with blood. The commode was sticky with a "red substance." The bathroom was literally covered with blood. While no body was found, it was theorized by some that the body had been butchered in the bathroom and perhaps then run through a meat grinder. At that time, Dr. Ruben Santos was the assistant medical examiner. He agreed that there was enough blood to indicate a butchering. Dr. Robert Hausman, the medical examiner, was out of the country at the time of the occurrence. He disagreed that there had been a butchering, saying he believed from police photographs that there was not enough blood. He also discarded the theory that a body was slowly run through a meat grinder and then flushed down the hotel bathroom commode. He projected the theory that the woman had given birth and the blood came from that, a theory that Frank Castillon has never agreed with. And then what would explain a bullet hole in the chair and the wall if this is what had taken place? No, Frank Castillon still stands firmly by his belief that there was definitely enough blood to indicate a butchering took place in room 636.

Checking out any clues they could find, Detectives Castillon and his partner, Bob Holt, discovered the suitcase they found in the room had been purchased on February 3, just prior to the time the man going under the name of Albert Knox had registered at the hotel. It was bought at the San Antonio Trunk and Gift Company at 211 Alamo Plaza, by a man who had used a personalized check of a Mr. John J. McCarthy. Mr. McCarthy turned out to be the stepfather of a Walter Emerick, the real name of "Albert Knox." The detectives then checked local restaurants to find the source of the cheese, wine, and sardines. When they visited Schilo's Delicatessen, at 424 E.Commerce Street, they learned a man, later ascertained to be Emerick, had dined with a "blonde woman" and had purchased $12.80 of take-out food, including the cheese and sardines. He had used a similar check to the one used to pay for the suitcase at Alamo Trunk. When questioned about the "John J. McCarthy" who signed the check, a restaurant employee surprised the officers by answering, "Oh, Mr. McCarthy didn't sign the check, it was his stepson, Walter something or other . . . I believe it is Urick. The McCarthys are regular customers." Evidently, the restaurant management recognized Mr. McCarthy's stepson and didn't want to make a big deal over his signing his stepfather's check.

Now suspecting a forgery case, District Attorney's investigator M. R. Nugent, who had joined Castillon in his investigations, went to the hot check section where he learned that "Walter Urick" was really "Walter Emerick," and a forgery charge had indeed been filed against him only the past week. Emerick was Mrs. John J. McCarthy's son by a previous marriage. He had had a previous forgery record and had served time. Fed up, apparently, with her son's habits, his mother had accused her son of taking fifty personalized checks on January 17. Learning that Emerick had a previous police record, fingerprints expert Captain A. M. Davenport matched up the fingerprints found in room 636 of the Gunter with those of Emerick's police record. The police finally had a suspect!

A statewide alert went out for Walter Emerick, a thirty-seven-year-old unemployed accountant. But just hours later, the police were to come to the end . . . the end of a dead-end street.

Sandor Ambrus, Jr., a security guard at the St. Anthony Hotel, located just a block away from the Gunter, became suspicious of one tenant who had checked into the hotel under the name of "Robert Ashley" on Tuesday. Arousing his suspicions was the fact that Ashley had not allowed the maids to enter the room to clean it.

Ambrus called in city and county officers and they went to room 536 at the St. Anthony. (Checks with that hotel revealed the man who signed in as Ashley had tried to rent room number 636 at the St. Anthony! When he found it was already occupied, he settled for room 536.)

Detective Castillon was with the security guard and asked him to use his key to unlock the door, fearing a sudden knock on the door might upset the man, who was thought to be armed. The guard was quite nervous, according to Castillon, and jangled the keys against the door, thus alerting the occupant. A shot rang out from within the room! Detective Castillon said he pushed the door open and was the first to reach the man, who had shot himself in the temple. He was still clutching his .22 caliber pistol. The detective asked him if he had killed anyone at the Gunter Hotel, but the man could only make a few "gurgling noises" before he expired.

In the St. Anthony room, a shirt was found which had been washed or rinsed out in an effort to remove blood stains. Also, cigars of the same brand as those found in the Gunter room were among the effects. And, of course, as police had no doubt, "Ashley's" fingerprints matched those found in Gunter room 636.

To this day, no body has ever been found. Police were never able to match fingerprints which were lifted from the room. No woman was ever reported to be missing. One police theory is that she may have been a prostitute.

One interesting twist did come to light during the investigation, when two sales clerks in a downtown department store later identified Emerick as the man who had come into the store and ordered a very large meat grinder!

At the time all this occurred, there was a lot of downtown construction going on, and green dye, used to color cement, was found on Emerick's shoes. One theory remains alive that he may have entombed parts of his victim in still-wet cement at one of the downtown construction projects.

The case is still open. No body has ever been discovered. The murderer, if indeed there was a murder, was dead by his own hand. A homicide detective was heard to say, "The best case we have is malicious mischief over $50. It took a couple of hundred dollars just to get the room clean," he added.

When we visited the room, we found it to be a small inside room, very close to the elevator. We were told the original room 636 had been divided into two rooms so what we saw was not the original crime scene. And, of course, all drapes, furnishings, carpets, etc. have been replaced. Only the tiny octagonal tiles, so popular in years past, in the bathroom, are original to the room . . . and though we looked very, very closely, there were no bloodstains to be seen on them!

Recent chats with members of the hotel's executive staff have revealed that there have been some unusual "happenings" from time to time in the famous landmark.

An executive who has been there for some time says that a woman in "ghostly garb" has been seen a number of times in the vicinity of room 636 where the activity took place. Two security guards reported sightings at different times, usually very late at night. On at least two occasions, hotel guests have been awakened by loud hammering noises in the rooms adjacent to theirs. When security guards were summoned to investigate, the rooms next door to the complainants were found to be unoccupied. The guards would check around, then leave, go back downstairs, and the noises would resume with no explanation.

Former staff member Jackie Contreras, who worked in the sales office and whose word we would certainly accept, said in 1990 she had a very frightening experience. She had gone to check on a room that had been made ready for some very important hotel clients. She went to the door and knocked. When no one answered, she opened the door with her passkey. The room was pitch black. She thought this rather strange, since the maids customarily would draw the drapes to allow sunlight to come into a room that had been made ready for guests. As she groped in the darkness for the light switch, she said the light coming in from the hallway revealed a "woman standing in the room. She was looking straight at me, her hands reaching towards me. She looked very old, and stooped, and was white as a sheet. She was wearing a long white gown." Jackie said she backed out fast, closing the door behind her. She went down to the lobby and told the people at the desk they must have given her the key to an occupied room. They assured her this was not so; the room was not occupied, as the maid had just finished making it ready for new occupants. She said as she thinks of it now, she is fully convinced the woman she saw was a ghost, and she still gets cold chills whenever she recalls that afternoon and the woman she saw in that dark, dark room.

At Christmas time, 1990, a group of the hotel employees gathered together to celebrate at an informal Christmas party up in the ballroom. One of those in attendance took some photographs of the gathering. One developed photo showed an extra personage in the picture . . . someone showed up with the group, who was not of the group . . . and nobody knows who it was, except another human form is very visible in the picture.

So there you are . . . an old and venerable hotel, situated in the very heart of historic San Antonio! The remarkable hostelry has been the scene of many gala balls, elegant gatherings, memorable speeches, and visits by the rich and famous. It also has the distinction of having a certain aura of mystery contained within those old walls. It is a wonderful hotel . . . a great place to dine in style . . . to spend a night, or a long vacation. And what is more . . . they won't charge you a penny extra for room 636!

The Menger Hotel . . .
Hauntingly Intriguing

The oldest hotel in San Antonio, the historic Menger, peacefully occupies a frontage on Alamo Plaza. In fact, the hotel is thought to be the oldest hostelry in America still operating in its original form. It is certainly one of the most charming! And, for good measure, it is said to include a ghost or two! But more about that later . . . .

Mr. William Menger, the builder, was an enterprising young brewer who was reputed to have made the "best beer west of the Mississippi." A natural extension of his first business, a tavern, was an inn to provide lodgings for his customers. Some of the early history of the hotel is rather sketchy, but it is logical to assume the intact basement walls, two to three feet thick, of hard-cut rock, provided the right

place to store hops and malt, imported from New York for this, one of the first breweries in Texas.

History also indicates the Alamo Madre Ditch, which forms one of the several existing tunnels beneath the original building, was once used for chilling the beer made on the spot. It was in the sub-basement or lower cellar of the building that the renegade Apache, Geronimo, is reputed to have been held prisoner for a time before being transported to a reservation. Today, in this most mysterious part of the hotel, there is a steel door with a metal bar and two padlocks. Behind the door is a ten-by-twelve-foot rock-walled room with an arched ceiling. This room, in spite of its strong security, contains nothing. Perhaps it is where Geronimo was held. And perhaps the woeful sounds that maintenance men have reported hearing are echoes of the mournful chants that the Indian made as he endured captivity. (Or perhaps, they are just wind drafts whistling through the old basement!)

When Mr. Menger decided to expand his small inn, he did it with great flair! People from far and wide came to the grand opening on February 2, 1859, and they've been beating a path to its doors ever since!

Mrs. Franz Stumpf wrote in her book *San Antonio's Menger* that the hotel "witnessed exciting events preceding the Civil War, shared the tragedies of that war and bore the trials of Reconstruction, sheltered the various artists who contributed their talents to San Antonio's cultural growth, inspired writers, honored military heroes and presidents . . . its fortunes rose and fell and rose again with those of the citizens of San Antonio."

Old ledgers and registration books reveal a veritable "Who's Who" of notable guests. Presidents William Howard Taft, William McKinley, U. S. Grant, Benjamin Harrison, Dwight Eisenhower, and Richard Nixon all have signed the guest register. Great opera and stage stars such as Sarah Bernhardt, Lillie Langtry, Anna Held, Sir Harry Lauder, Maude Adams, Richard Mansfield, and Beverly Sills enjoyed the Menger hospitality. There were the famous writers and poets, Sidney Lanier, Oscar Wilde, and "O. Henry" (William Sidney Porter). General John Pershing, Texas Ranger Captain Leander McNelly, Buffalo Bill Cody, General Phillip Sheridan, and John L. Sullivan were also Menger visitors. Roy Rogers and his charming wife, Dale Evans, stayed there so often that the hotel has named the Roy Rogers Suite in their honor.

Theodore (Teddy) Roosevelt, who is said to have done much of his recruiting for his famous Rough Riders from the convivial atmosphere of the Menger bar, was another famous guest back in 1898. One hotel manager who was convinced the hotel was "hauntingly alive" says he knows Teddy's ghost has come back several times to visit the Menger bar.

Maintenance men have spoken of doors that will not stay closed although they were locked, and relocked. They have also told of hearing musical sounds and marching footsteps in various parts of the hotel.

We read an article in an old *Express News* that stated guests had reported seeing a "woman in blue" walking silently through the hallways on several occasions. Historian David Bowser wrote about this particular lady in his *Guidebook to Some Out of the Way Historical Sights in the City of the Alamo*: "There are a host of interesting stories about this grand old hotel. One of the most fascinating and little known of these is that of the Lady in Blue.

"For some time, there have been rumors of odd occurrences in a certain second-floor room in one of the old sections of the hotel. The door to the room faces on a long, dimly lit hallway where the wooden floorboards creak as you walk over them. The rear of the room has long floor-to-ceiling windows. Outside, there is a little balcony with a green painted railing of iron grillwork. From these windows, you can look down upon the famous Patio Garden of the hotel.

"Several of the hotel's personnel assigned to this room have experienced bizarre incidents . . . strange noises, room lights flicking on and off inexplicably, doors closing of their own accord, and a general feeling as though someone was watching."

Mr. Bowser continues: "The most eerie incident occurred one day while one of the maids was routinely cleaning the room. She had a strong feeling as though someone was in there with her. Thinking it was one of the guests, she turned and was stunned to see a woman in an old-fashioned long blue dress sitting calmly in a chair a few feet away. The maid described the apparition as an attractive looking woman with blondish shoulder length hair, worn in a style of the 1930s or '40s. She also related that the figure in the chair appeared real but had a very odd look about her because of the way she was dressed, and also, as the awe-struck worker gazed at the woman, the figure suddenly disappeared. The maid told her story with conviction and sincerity. She was not kidding around . . . not in the least.

"So it would appear the Old Menger has a ghost. Some of the staff are understandably reluctant to talk about such things from a business standpoint. However, it seems the ghost would attract more business than it would repel."

Mr. Bowser concluded his article with the provocative question, "Who was the Lady in Blue in life, and why does her spirit haunt this old hotel room?" (Romanticists that we are . . . we'd like to think she is remembering a grand ball she enjoyed at the hotel while wearing her blue gown . . . or maybe she is waiting for a romantic tryst, wearing her lover's favorite color!)

One maid, who has been there for some years, also believes the hotel is haunted. She says she has never seen the woman in blue, but knows of people who have. She did know of the best known of the Menger spirits . . . a lady whose restless spirit roams the long halls on the third floor of the original building. This most-sighted ghost has always worn a full, floor length skirt, and has a scarf or a bandanna tied around her head. A long necklace of beads has been seen dangling around her neck, and sometimes she wears an apron. This ghost is believed to be that of Sallie White, a chambermaid who worked at the Menger in 1876. People who have seen her believe she likes to return to the place where she spent so much time making beds, cleaning, dusting, and tidying up the rooms. She worked hard and was well liked and appreciated by the hotel management. Unfortunately, her life was cut short on March 28, 1876, when, while working at the hotel, she was shot by her husband (he must not have been a very nice fellow). She hung on for two painful, agonizing days before she expired.

In the lobby of the hotel one may see an interesting display of old hotel ledgers. One of them is opened to an entry by one Frederick Hahn. Into the "cash paid" column, there is written: "To cash paid for coffin for Salie White, col'd chambermaid, deceased, murdered by her husband, shot March 28, died March 30, $25 for coffin, and $7 for grave, total, $32."

We are told that even now some of the maids prefer to work in pairs, particularly in the old section of the hotel, because they do believe in the hauntings.

Recently we were told one of the young ladies in the hotel sales office encountered Sallie while making the rounds of the hotel. She is said to have been "somewhat unnerved" when she returned to her desk.

While Sallie White is probably the most often sighted ghost, we also learned of still another . . . .

A very famous guest who always stayed at the Menger when he visited San Antonio was Captain Richard King, founder of the famous King Ranch, south of San Antonio, at Kingsville. The King Suite is still furnished with period furniture used during his stays there, including the old four-poster bed complete with canopy, in which he passed away. The Captain died at dusk in August of 1885 of unknown causes, in his room at the hotel. He loved the hotel so much that his funeral service was conducted in the big front parlor.

A young man with a local security company, who once worked as a guard at the Menger, told us that one night, when he was patrolling the hallways of the older section of the hotel, he saw a man going down the hall quite late at night. "He was dressed like Colonel Sanders of fried chicken fame" . . . wearing old-fashioned western type clothing, including a string tie and broad brimmed black hat. The guard said he followed the gentleman and as he came to a turning in the hallway he did not turn . . . he just literally disappeared! The guard went down to the lobby and asked the other guard on duty if he had seen the mysterious visitor. He had not. Our friend also told of several times when he was on duty at night and got into the elevator in the older section, no matter what floor he punched, the elevator would always stop at the third floor.

A visit last year with one of the executives at the front desk revealed still another interesting facet to the hotel. Everyone knows, of course, that Teddy Roosevelt spent at lot of time at the hotel in 1898, when he was in San Antonio recruiting and training his Rough Riders. It seems there was a little bell at the front desk, which visitors used to ring for service. It was disconnected some time back and yet, periodically, it would still ring, quite loudly! The desk staff decided it must just be Teddy's ghost, demanding the usual prompt service he enjoyed when he used to hang out at the Menger. It even went off during our interview with the front desk personnel, so we can attest to its performance! We have learned, however, since a very recent remodeling job in the front desk area, the bell has been removed, so it is no longer available for Teddy to ring. Must be very frustrating for the spirit, but more peaceful for the employees!

We are sure there are other interesting "ghostly" happenings at the hotel, because it has had such a colorful history. It is one of those places which recalls the elegant days of the Deep South when cotton was king, Men were MEN and women didn't give a hoot about Women's Lib, and life was lived in a gracious and relaxed manner. Its walls could tell many stories of life, love, death, intrigue, and adventure if only walls could talk. A quote from the writer Oliver St. John Gagarty sums up the history of the lovely old landmark to date: "A house outlives its owner, and from old cities and houses there can emanate a reviving memory of men who died for liberty or sang for joy of life." We think it's all there . . . at the Menger.

Shadows at El Tropicana

The former El Tropicana, near the Municipal Auditorium, is now a newly refurbished Holiday Inn. Our stories concern the hotel before it changed management.

When a gentleman we know, who now works at another hotel, was a very young man, he worked at the El Tropicana Hotel as a bellman. He told us about the time, many years ago, when he became an overnight believer in ghosts. It was about 2 a.m. and he had been called to deliver ice to one of the upper floor rooms. As he got off the elevator and started down the long hallway he saw a man "dressed all in black, walking towards me." He said the figure was "tall and menacing" and was wearing some sort of short cape over his shoulders and a round brimmed Spanish type hat. The clothes did not look like they fitted into the current era at all. Our acquaintance said as the man approached, and then passed him, he couldn't get up the nerve to look straight at him, so he looked down at the floor as the figure passed by. But then, after he had gone just a few more steps, he looked back. There was no one to be seen. He said if the man had entered a room along the corridor, he would certainly have heard a door being opened, and the apparition, if that is what it was, had not had enough time to have walked down the length of the hallway before he looked back. He said he left his ice in the room to which he had been summoned, but he refused to go upstairs in the hotel during the rest of his duty hours that night. Even today, he says he gets cold chills when he recalls that evening.

Still another time, several years later, he said it was around 1974, the former bellman had worked his way up the corporate ladder to an executive position at the hotel. One evening, very late, after the El Fontana Club at the hotel had closed for the evening, a group of six or eight employees were gathered around a table for a late night visit before going home. It was around 2 a.m. The talk seemed to center on ghosts and strange night happenings among the conversationalists. Suddenly, he said, there appeared in front of them a "big black shadow in the shape of a huge man." They all saw it, and it was definitely something "not of this world." The party is said to have broken up in a hurry!

Now, we don't know for sure, but one source told us that he had heard that the El Tropicana building, which is located right on the banks of the San Antonio River, was built over the site of an old Indian burial ground in 1962. We have heard no word of any recent other-worldly appearances. Since the hotel changed management, the spirits must have moved away to another location.

The Country Spirit Named David

On the main street of the small town of Boerne, north of San Antonio, there is a charming restaurant called the Country Spirit, located at 707 South Main. It is located in an old house, which was one of Boerne's first two-storied homes. It was designed by a French architect named Lamatt. In 1872, soon after its construction, it was sold to Rudolph Carstarjen. A large home, it was known as The Mansion for many years.

During the early 1900s it served for several years as an annex to the Phillip Manor Hotel across the street. At this time a drugstore was located in a portion of the ground floor. Later, Mrs. Augusta Phillip used the mansion as her personal residence until she married Mr. Henry Graham.

In the early 1950s it was sold to the Gilman Hall family and they resided in the house until it was converted into a restaurant in the late 1970s. After several other owners came and went, it was purchased by Sue Martin in 1984 and com-

pletely remodeled with great care towards preserving its architectural and historical integrity. When she opened her restaurant she renamed it the Country Spirit, and herein lies a story.

Mrs. Martin insists the place is haunted, and according to former occupants, it has been the favorite spot for a spirit named David for many years.

Several psychics who have visited the place have told the owner that the ghost should be referred to as "David." He seems to prefer the upstairs men's restroom, located in one of the old bathrooms where there is an old-fashioned bathtub. In deference to him, they have placed a little pillow with "David" embroidered on it in the tub so he can comfortably rest and feel at home there!

The story goes that David was a local orphan boy in his early teens. Having no family, he sort of took up with the people who resided in the mansion, and the cook there would often give him hand-outs from the kitchen. He was also allowed to play with the children of the household. There was a driveway, used for buggies then, at the side of the house, and that is where the children liked to play. David either fell or was pushed down on the driveway, most likely by accident. He sustained injuries from which he could not recover and soon died. This event is said to have taken place sometime in the 1890s.

Mrs. Martin said many things continue to happen in the restaurant which convince her and her employees that the spirit is still very much around. She has witnessed a candle moving unassisted from one side of a table to the opposite side. Once, as a local gentleman sat at the bar, which is located in the rear portion of the building, four glasses suddenly flew off the shelves, one at a time. The man, who works as a security guard at a nearby place of business, said they "did not fall off . . . they were thrown" . . . and he added he had not been drinking when he witnessed this!

The beer spigot has been known to turn on by itself, and spoons have flown across the kitchen! Recently, all the lights in the bar went out. They did not come back on, but had to be turned on at the switch.

Mrs. Martin said she had been told that before she owned the place, there had been a small apartment upstairs. The occupants had reported hearing people "laughing and partying" downstairs, but when they checked, there was never anyone there.

Frequently, she reports, there are footsteps heard in the upstairs portion of the restaurant. This usually happens late at night after the place has closed.

David seems to enjoy the sort of pranks that a young person would, and evidently he just doesn't want to be forgotten. The food is still excellent, as served from the kitchen of the Country Spirit, and after all, that's what attracted David to the house in the first place.

Ye Kendall Inn

A favorite dining, shopping, and weekending place, within a short and pleasant driving distance from San Antonio, is the historic Ye Kendall Inn in the little town of Boerne.

The place has a fascinating past, as do many of South Texas' old landmarks, and for good measure, there's a ghost story or two! More about that later on . . . .

On April 23, 1859, Erastus and Sarah Reed purchased the five-acre plot of ground from John Jones. They paid $200, which was a goodly sum in those days, for the land. The property extended down to the Cibolo Creek. There was, and is, a hand dug well on the place which is twenty feet deep and has provided ice cold, fresh water for many, many years.

The Reeds had a native cut-rock house built, which reflected the Southern Colonial architecture so popular at that time. What today is the center section of the Inn is the portion they constructed. The sturdy walls were twenty inches thick, and there was a long front porch with a southerly exposure, allowing maximum summer breezes to enter the house.

There was also a tunnel that extended from the cellar of the building and evidently connected the hotel with a building about a block away. It is believed the underground passageway was built as a protection from the hostile bands of Indians who were still wandering in the area at the time the house was built. The stairway down to the cellar is also of native hewn stone. We do not know for sure whether the Reeds built the cellar, or whether a subsequent owner was responsible for having that work done.

In the late 1850s there were no hotels in the area for travelers and so a number of Boerne residents would rent their rooms out to transients. The Reeds followed the custom of their neighbors and also rented out their spare rooms.

Later on a man named Harry W. Chipman leased the Reed property and he also rented accommodations to horsemen and stagecoach passengers. The grounds, which now are occupied by the Courtyard Restaurant served as a wagonyard for ranchers who kept their cattle penned in what is now the city park just across the street from the Kendall Inn. This was one of the gathering points for cattle drivers going up the long Chisholm trail to the railroads in Kansas.

In 1869 Colonel Henry C. King and his wife, Jean Adams King, bought the building. For a while the Colonel served as a State Senator, riding back and forth to Austin on horseback. During his absences Mrs. King ran the "King Place" as it was then known.

In 1878 C. J. Rountree and W. L. Wadsworth of Dallas bought the King property and gave it still another name, the Boerne Hotel. At this time the two long expansive wings on either side of the original building were added to accommodate a much larger clientele.

Finally, four years later, in 1882, an English couple, Edmund and Selina King, came to Boerne and bought the hotel. A short time after they took possession of the property, Edmund King was tragically killed in a hunting accident in back of the hotel on September 26, 1882.

Throughout the 1880s the Boerne Hotel served as an authentic stagecoach inn, where horses were changed, and travelers rested. Finally, it was purchased by Dr. H. D. Barnitz. He renamed the place Ye Kendall Inn in honor of George W. Kendall for whom Kendall County is named.

Still other owners entered the scene in 1922 when Robert L. and Maude M. Hickman owned the place. They greatly modernized the building, adding numerous private bathrooms. They owned the place until 1943.

Coming on down the line to the present, the owners today are Ed and Vicki Schleyer, who purchased the inn in April of 1982. They spent much time and money restoring the place into the charming building that greets visitors today, with its polished hardwood floors, fine mantels surmounting the original fireplaces, and lovely woodwork. They also added an absolutely wonderful (for the ladies, at least!) clothing shop called Victoria's Boutique.

Now, Vicki Schleyer says she is sure there's a ghost . . . or maybe two or three, who live at the inn, or at least stop off frequently as guests. She didn't have an inkling the place might be haunted until after she had signed the final papers. Then her realtor, Barbara Grinnan, just kind of let the information slip that there just "might be a ghost around." Schleyer did not give it much thought until she and a helper were busy getting ready for a catering job, and she suddenly heard heavy footsteps treading overhead. She asked her co-worker if she heard anything, and the lady told her, no, she didn't. Vicki still heard the noises, a measured tread of footsteps, and so she went upstairs to investigate. Her search resulted in her finding nothing there at all!

Then, in the 1980s, while the place was being restored, a worker fell through the floor as he tried to install a bathroom fixture. The claw legs kept falling off of an old bathtub. Strange things just kept happening in that same room, for no apparent reason.

Vicki's husband, Ed Schleyer, is a taxidermist. She said he chose to work in the building, upstairs, one night. He kept hearing doors opening and then slamming shut. He knew he was alone in the building and all the entrances were securely locked. But the noises kept on and on until he packed up and left, vowing never to work there again at night!

Employees in the restaurant have reported crystal prisms have fallen off a chandelier, a doorknob between the restaurant and the shop will often rattle, and electricity sometimes just won't turn on . . . all for no apparent reason.

In 1991 a hotel guest ate lunch in the restaurant and then took a short stroll around the grounds. When he returned, the man asked Ed Shane, a staff member, if there were any ghosts around. Ed told him he had heard a lot of stories and rather believed there just might be. The visitor then went on to describe the spirit he had seen as an elderly woman, her hair done up in an old-fashioned bun, who was wearing Victorian clothes. She told him her name was "Sarah," he said. Shane told him that the first owner's wife was named Sarah Reed!

When Vicki Schleyer bought the house, her realtor told her one of the rooms seemed to have more spirit activity than any others. She believes it is a room they call the Marcella Booth room. Marcella was born at the inn. As a young woman, she was very lovely; there are pictures of her on the walls, including one of her posing as a Duchess in one of San Antonio's elegant Fiesta Coronations. Booth still lives in Boerne, an elderly but still active woman. The room has a pencil-poster bed, and beautiful drapes covering the large windows. Who lived, or stayed there, that might cause the room to appear haunted, is not known. Often when innkeeper Rick Villarreal goes up to check on rooms prior to new guests checking in he finds that room looks as if someone had just sat on the bed . . . and the bed coverings have to be smoothed out.

Vicki Schleyer enjoys her ghostly visitors. Last Halloween she went so far as to dress like a "wraith" in an old wedding dress she discovered while renovating the house (probably a gown that had belonged to a former owner that had been tucked away in a box and forgotten) and play the part of the "Spirit of Ye Kendall Inn." She says the ghosts (there is probably more than one) are friendly and benevolent, and she hopes they continue to stay there, enjoying the hospitality of Ye Kendall Inn!

The Lady in the Choir Loft

At the corner of Alamo and Wickes streets, in the King William Historic District, there's an old brick church building. It used to be called the Alamo Methodist Church and served the Methodists in the area for many years until 1976 when the congregation had dwindled to the point it was no longer practical to maintain a church in that area. The building, which was constructed in 1913 in what was a popular architectural style of the day, called the "Mission Style," has two bell towers and twin steps and doors at either side of the front. There are lovely Tiffany windows still in place, and the ceilings are of white-washed punched tin. The upper area was the sanctuary of the church, while the basement level housed the Sunday School rooms. The building is listed on the National Register of Historic Places.

As a Bicentennial project, Bill and Marcia (Marcie) Larsen bought the building after it was secularized and converted it into a dinner theatre, which was known as the Church Dinner

Theatre. This was when I first became acquainted with the place, the productions, and the genial owners. The theatrical productions were in the former chapel, and dinner, always a sumptuous affair, was offered in the basement level.

For a time, Jerry Pollock operated the theatre portion (from 1984 to 1987). Then the Larsens just operated the restaurant and for some time the old sanctuary was used for an occasional meeting, film, or lecture.

In April of 1991 the Larsens got back into the theatre business, and productions have been going on since that date and have been quite well received.

Now the building itself is interesting enough to pay a visit . . . and the historical district in which it is located is also intriguing . . . but what really sets it apart is there is a really, truly, "resident ghost" as well! In fact, there may be more than one spirit as so many strange happenings occur from time to time it might wear out just one ghost to do it all! From just about the time the Larsens purchased the building in 1976, a figure of a woman, dressed in Victorian dress of the late 1800s or early 1900s, has been seen in the former choir loft. She is always dressed in white. Her sightings have been noted by many performers and stage crew members over the years. She always appears in just that area, but unseen occurrences take place all over the building, from the lower level kitchens to the upper areas of the building!

The Larsens are quite willing to share their experiences with visitors to the restaurant. They say that the mysterious lady in white seems to frequent the building most often when a play is in rehearsal or production. This has given the Larsens the idea she just might possibly be the spirit of the late Miss Margaret Gething. Gething was a charming and beautiful woman who had been a singer and actress on the legitimate stage during the early days of this century. Her home was only a block away from the church, on Guenther Street, and she had quite possibly attended services or special events at the old church during her lifetime. And oh, how she had loved the stage! Since no one who formerly attended the church as a member of the congregation can identify the woman as a previous choir member, the Gething theory is as good as any other that has been projected thus far.

Although the figure has only been seen in the choir loft, other things that are unexplainable do happen in the building.

Sudden cold spots are discernible. Lights sometimes go on and off for no reason. In the kitchen, in the basement level, cooks have been shoved against the refrigerator. Dishes, washed and draining on drainboards, have suddenly been placed back in the dishwater by unseen hands. Doors open and close and lock and unlock themselves. Unusual noises continue to persist. The Larsens aren't sure if just one young lady ghost could do all these things!

Brian Cobb, until recently the theatre director, was very willing to talk to us about some of his experiences. The former choir loft, up above the entry door into the chapel, is now used to house light and sound equipment for the productions. Sometimes after everything is carefully set up, the technicians take a break. When they return, they'll find electric cords unplugged, or tied in knots, or things disturbed in other ways. Whether the ghost is upset, or just playful, is anyone's guess!

Cobb doesn't seem to share Larsen's belief the lady was a former actress. He thinks maybe she is someone who had something to do with the church, or a person who might have lived on the site prior to the church's being built in 1913. One thing for sure, she has a favorite dress! She's always dressed in white, with a V neck, puffed sleeves, and a fitted bodice. That's about all that can be seen of her up in the choir loft.

Cobb told about one time when he was at the theatre during rehearsal and was sitting out in one of the pews (now used as theatre seats) watching the actors on stage go through their lines. Suddenly, he heard a husky feminine voice whisper in his ear ... "Brian ... Brian." Of course, no one was there. Another time, the other worldly lady begged "help me! please, help me!" This time Brian's partner, Paul Gaedke, who was with him in the auditorium, heard the voice as well.

Once, during an actual performance, the audience and cast were caught by surprise, when the female voice of an unseen singer was heard singing in the area where the audience was seated. This was during an especially quiet moment in the drama! Thus far, Cobb has only heard the ghost ... unlike some of his performers, he has not seen her. He says he wishes he could glimpse her, because he thinks she is a good and benevolent, although lonely, little spirit. He thinks the place has "good energy, or vibes ... because of her presence."

Brian said his father often came to the theatre to do some volunteer work for him, and whenever he would arrive at the building, his watch would stop running. As soon as he left, it would start running again! No explanation, of course.

During the summer of 1990 a tourist couple named Barbara and Edward Kulis from out of state came to the restaurant to eat. Their interest was caught as they read the write-up about the "ghost" on the Alamo Restaurant's menu. Barbara told the Larsens she was inclined toward being psychic, and would certainly like to see the upstairs portion of the building. Now, there was no production or rehearsal going on right then, and the upstairs air-conditioner was shut off. It was HOT! Even so, as they climbed the narrow steps from the restaurant level to the theatre portion, Barbara said she had sudden cold chills. Her husband, who does not believe in psychic phenomena, also felt suddenly cold.

The pair wandered around the theatre a few minutes and then Barbara asked Ed to take a photo of the choir loft and entry door beneath it with his poloroid camera. He took two shots of the area. As soon as the photographs developed, an apparition of someone clad in a white dress could be seen. One photo is far clearer than the other. The Kulises had not seen any figure as they stood in the old chapel, but the sensitive film was able to capture a good likeness of the ghost. In the clearer of the two pictures, the head is just a fuzzy bit of white mist, but one can clearly make out a torso with a V neck, puffed sleeves, nipped in waist, and full puffed skirt. The figure is in the center of the doorway, but slightly rising, as the "exit" sign over the door is obliterated by the figure. The photos are framed now and hanging in the restaurant.

Barbara Kulis told the Larsens she was never frightened during her visit but she definitely felt a "presence" and only wished she could have somehow helped the spirit.

At present, Bill and Marcie are running the Alamo Church Restaurant and the theatrical productions with guest companies and directors appearing there. Marcie, an ebullient, bouncy, friendly lady, and Bill, tall and sophisticated, are perfect hosts to their many restaurant clients . . . as they continue to serve good food and good drama in their old church locale. Evidently the "lady in white," whoever she is, enjoys their hospitality as well . . . because she's definitely still around!

Spirits Come Back to the Settlement Inn

The thriving little community of Leon Springs is just a short drive northwest of San Antonio on IH 10. An immigrant from Germany, Max Aue, founded the community back in the 1850s.

Aue spent his first year in Texas visiting in Sisterdale, and then in 1852 he joined the Texas Rangers under Captain Owen Shaw's leadership. Aue was cited for his excellent marksmanship and bravery during the three years he served with the prestigious law enforcement agency. When he resigned from the Rangers in 1855 he received 640 acres as payment for his services. This land became the foundation of holdings he increased to over 20,000 acres prior to his death in 1903.

In 1857 Aue married nineteen-year-old Emma Toepperwein, whose family had arrived in Texas from Germany at the same time Aue had arrived. The Toepperweins had settled up in Fredericksburg. When Emma and her family visited Aue in 1856 at his Leon Springs homestead, romance blossomed. A year later Emma and Max were married.

Aue established the Leon Springs Supply Company, a general store in the building that until very recently housed the restaurant known as the Settlement Inn. There was a general store in the front room of the two-story rock structure, and a post office in the back room. The little building also had a cellar as well. Mr. and Mrs. Aue made their home in the upstairs living quarters.

Because the stagecoach lines used Aue's store as a horse-changing station and rest stop, he built the Leon Springs Hotel across the patio from his general store and post office building. The stage route ran between San Diego, California, and San Antonio, and was the longest regular stage route in the United States. Depending on what direction the travelers were going, the Leon Springs station was the first, or the next to last, stop on the twenty-five day journey.

The Aue's hotel became a popular place for visitors from throughout the United States to stop over. One gentleman, Lorenzo Hyatt of New York, met the Aue's daughter, Clara, while visiting in the area. A romance developed and Clara married Hyatt and moved back to New York with him.

After Max Aue's death, employees of the family enterprises continued to occupy the small rock house and adjacent hotel until 1957 when both became vacant. Then in 1973 the property was leased to Steven Spence, a much decorated U.S. Army Ranger who had served in Vietnam. Spence combined his dual interests in good food and historical buildings and undertook extensive renovations of the store and hotel. The former store building was named the Settlement Inn and became a very popular restaurant.

During the past six or seven years, many people, some of them employees at the Settlement, have sworn that they have seen the specters of Max and Emma Aue. The spirits seem to want to cling to their old home and hotel.

Denice Hardy, a former restaurant manager, said Mrs. Aue seemed to call most often at the former store and post office areas of the building, while Max was first seen at one of the hotel windows. It seems that late one afternoon a member of the Sheriff's Department drove by the hotel and chanced to glimpse a figure standing at a hotel window. Thinking it was an intruder, he called for backup. When other officers arrived, they could find no one there. A few days later the officer who had seen the physical likeness of a man in the window was flipping through the pages of the Settlement Inn's flier and noticed a picture of Max Aue. "Why, that's the man I saw in the window," he exclaimed.

Hardy believes the reason the Aue's return to their old home is that they were buried in undesignated graves across IH 10 from their old homestead. When that site was earmarked for a community center, the bodies of the pair were exhumed and reinterred in Mission Park North, a large cemetery just south of Leon Springs. It was just at that time that all the strange things started to happen.

There have been reports of footsteps being heard walking across the upstairs floors. Hardy said the visiting spirits also were heard pounding on a typewriter located in the former upstairs living quarters on three consecutive nights. One employee told Hardy he had seen a ghostly figure at least seven times.

Some people who have sighted the female ghost say she must be the spirit of Emma Aue. They've described the apparition as being from five feet six inches, to five feet nine inches tall, and she wears a full and flowing gown. (Probably the more frightened the viewer, the taller the ghost appears to be!) She's reported to have turned chairs around, and sometimes she took the time to light all the kerosene lamps in the restaurant before she took her leave. Hardy recalls once going down in the cellar to change clothes. She felt someone touch her shoulder. Of course, when she looked around, no one was there. She said she got out of there, fast, "screaming bloody murder!"

It is said Emma Aue was killed by Indians. Maybe she comes back looking for her killers. We think she just enjoys visiting her old homestead.

The Settlement Inn property was recently sold and has just recently reopened as a Mexican restaurant called Nacho Mama's. We wonder if the new owners have heard any unexplained sneezing lately? The Aues may not yet be used to chili powder!

CHAPTER 3

Haunted Houses

HAUNTED HOUSES
Docia Williams

Some ghosts are known to frequently roam
Through a once beloved and treasured old home . . .
Where strangers now dwell, in their house, on their land.
(They don't know they're dead, they don't understand.)
So when nights grow dark, and silent and still
Their spirits come out in the cold and the chill . . . .
Searching to see if all is in place,
Wandering each room and checking each space,
Their footsteps are heard on stairway and floor.
Sometimes they'll open a window, or door;
If someone has altered the looks of a room,
It seems to fill them with sorrow, and gloom.
So if you move into a house old and dear,
There's one point to make most perfectly clear . . .
Leave it as is . . . so the spirits can rest . . .
Or they'll keep coming back to the place they loved best!

A Note About Haunted Houses

In 1955 I had a personal experience that convinced me there are such things as ghosts and haunted houses. My former husband, Stanley Southworth, was sent to England to be stationed with the United States Air Force at RAF Sculthorpe, in Norfolk County. Soon after our arrival, which was in May, we found lodgings in a lovely flat on the third floor of a famous manor house, Raynham Hall. It was the ancestral mansion of the Townshend family. At the time of our living there, both Lord and Lady Townshend were spending the summer in Switzerland, but I did become well acquainted with the Dowager Marchioness Gladys Townshend, who was the mother of the Marquess. She lived in London but often visited the estate, and it was on one of these visits that I met her, and we became friends. Later, I visited her in London.

From the time we moved in, I felt cold in the house, even though it was summer, and a nice warm one at that. I never felt at ease in the large flat and was especially uncomfortable in the bedroom. We had a number of friends who visited us that summer and they all expressed being uncomfortable in the place. I had to enter the Hall, as the manor was known, by the back doorway and go through a large entryway and then up a winding marble flight of stairs to my apartment. I was always very uncomfortable, but didn't really know why, as I went up the stairs.

Then one night, when my husband was away on a mission, I was sitting up in bed, reading some magazines and newspapers my mother had sent me from the States. It was rather late, and I had my mind on nothing more than my reading material. Suddenly, the door knob turned on the closed door into the bedroom, and I felt a draft of cold air pass my bed. There was an odor . . . I can best describe it like that of a root cellar or old damp basement. Then, the heavy velvet drapes along the wall of the room, which covered a series of windows, suddenly drew back, by themselves, and whatever it was that caused this to happen opened a closed pair of French doors opening onto a small balcony. I was so taken back, I was frozen, unable to move for a very long time. Later, when I mentioned what had happened to the old butler who worked in the manor house, he said, "Oh, it just must have been the Brown Lady, Mum." No other explanation, and I was unable to find out much else until I met Lady Gladys Townshend.

The ghost, which is one of England's most famous, has been around Raynham Hall for well over two hundred and fifty years. The manor house was built in 1620 by Inigo Jones and is a huge red brick building situated on a large estate overlooking a lake. The ghost, which I only "felt," has actually been seen . . . and photographed as well, by a number of people. I learned she is believed to be the spirit of Dorothy Walpole Townshend. Her portrait, which was sold along with other Townshend heirlooms at Christies in 1904, was said to picture a lovely young woman with large, shining eyes, dressed in brown with yellow trimmings and a large ruff around her neck, as was the style of the period in which she lived. It is said she looked lovely in ordinary light, but when seen in candlelight, the portrait took on a sinister appearance as the flesh seemed to shrink from her face and the eyes would disappear giving the portrait the look of a skull.

Dorothy Walpole came from a famous Norfolk family. Her father was Sir Robert Walpole, a member of Parliament, and her brother was the great Sir Robert Walpole, the first Prime Minister of England. When Dorothy was a very young girl, her father was appointed guardian of young Viscount Charles Townshend, whose father had died when Charles was just thirteen. This began a very sad romance. Dorothy fell in love with Charles, but her father forbade the match because he did not want it said he was trying to gain a family advantage by match-making his daughter to the wealthy young Townshend.

Lord Charles Townshend was married to the daughter of the Baron Pelham of Laughton, but she died young, in 1711. A year or so later he did marry his first love, Dorothy. But Dorothy's great disappointment in Charles being married to another had resulted in her loss of reasoning and reputation. She had had a rather shady affair with a known reprobate of the day, by the name of Lord Wharton. Wharton later had to flee the country, leaving a trail of creditors behind.

Evidently Charles Townshend did not know that Dorothy had previously been Wharton's mistress, before they were married, when she was twenty-six years of age. The Townshends became estranged, and Lord Townshend is said to have locked his beautiful wife in her apartments at Raynham so she would not again stray from the straight and narrow. The story goes that after such harsh treatment she died of a broken heart in 1726. Another story says she died of a broken neck, which was the result of a fall down the grand staircase at Raynham, while another more contemporary version says she died of smallpox. I don't know how she died, but I did visit her burial place in the little chapel on the grounds of the manor house, and I do feel she came into my bedroom on several occasions!

It must be remembered her brother was one of the most important men in England and her husband was also a wealthy and powerful man with no little influence in government. If the real cause of her death was concealed from the general public, this might explain the restive nature of her spirit.

No matter how she actually died, we do know that Dorothy's ghost has terrorized residents, visitors, and servants in the manor for the better part of two and a half centuries. Even royalty had a frightening encounter with the ghost! When George IV was Regent, he visited the Townshends and the Brown Lady frightened him out of his wits. His Royal Highness awakened his host in the middle of the night saying that a lady, dressed in brown, "with disheveled hair and a face of ashy paleness" had appeared at his bedside in the State Bedroom, and he vowed he wouldn't spend another hour in what he referred to as "this accursed house."

It was apparent that the Brown Lady's presence was not a social asset to the Townshends. Many great parties at which the most famous and aristocratic of noble families were invited were held there and the word was getting around that the ghost was pretty active. While I lived there, I was shown bullet holes in one room where a houseguest had shot at the apparition when it appeared at the foot of his bed.

The famous ghost was actually photographed, according to Lady Gladys Townshend, who told me of having had a houseparty there one weekend. A society photographer had taken photos of her along with some of her friends to later be printed in a society magazine. One photograph, which showed three ladies seated on a loveseat, revealed the figure of a woman standing behind the loveseat, with her hands resting on the back. She was dressed in a period gown, with a high ruff around her neck.

In 1936 Lady Townshend commissioned Mr. Indre Shira, a professional photographer, to take some interior photographs of the Hall. On the afternoon of Sept. 19, 1936, he and his assistant, a Mr. Provand, were taking flash light photos of the grand staircase. As the two photographers were working, suddenly they saw what was later described as a vaporous form which gradually took on the appearance of a woman draped in some light, transparent fabric. She came floating down the steps, and as she came closer, Mr. Provand aimed his camera and took what has since become a very famous picture. After the flash, the specter disappeared.

This photo later appeared in an issue of *Country Life Magazine* (Dec. 16, 1936) and then much later, the photo was reproduced in *Time Magazine* (Feb. 18, 1957). This same photo has been seen recently on several television shows dealing with the supernatural.

I guess I should feel fortunate that my initial acquaintanceship with ghosts should take place in such a famous old house, with a celebrity spirit! I must say, after only three months in the manor house, we decided to move to another address . . . less elegant, but certainly more peaceful.

From those early unnerving experiences at Raynham Hall, I became a believer . . . I know there is something out there that we do not understand, and therefore as I started to interview many of the people whose stories appear in this chapter, I did not doubt their veracity or their sincerity.

A well-known medium who has visited San Antonio several times, Elizabeth Paddon, stated that she believed that at least ten percent of all houses are in some way haunted. According to an article written by Nicki Frances McDaniel, which appeared in the July 22, 1990 issue of the *San Antonio Express News*, Paddon stated "sometimes when people don't believe in an afterlife, their spirits will stay around after they die because they don't know where else to go." She went on to say, "Some spirits stay around because they feel they have unfinished business or responsibilities to attend to. Other ghosts may not even realize they are dead, and are caught in a sort of limbo, neither here on earth nor in the light where they will find eternal rest. The latter is especially common in the case of suicides," she added. I also believe that when a will or some other wishes of the deceased were not carried out as desired, the restive spirit will return to haunt those who did not abide by their wishes. Sometimes they will return to a place where they were very unhappy, or where they died, especially if the death was sudden or violent.

Then, there are also ghosts who seem to come back to places where they knew great contentment and happiness. Perhaps they just can't quite break loose from a place they loved. Sometimes these spirits get really upset when someone remodels or changes a home they had designed and decorated, and they are pretty adamant about making this known. Still other spirits, the not-so-nice ones, return where they were happy, but because they have a selfish streak in them somewhere, they don't want the current occupants to be happy there, and they hope their constant harassment will be sufficiently unnerving that the occupants will move away. Most "household ghosts" are just nuisances and not at all harmful. Most of them are just pitifully unhappy lost spirits.

Ghosts don't just belong to "ancient history" either. Buildings can be haunted that are fairly new . . . since ghosts have no chronological order of appearance. Right here in San Antonio there are buildings of fairly recent construction that are already haunted. The spirits in those buildings haven't been gone all that long, so we might call them "apprentice spirits"! In some incidences in this book, we have personally known the living beings which are now referred to as ghostly occupants. Then too, a building can be haunted for years and years, and suddenly, for no apparent reason, the ghostly presence can disappear and never again reappear.

A friend of ours who is psychic, Sam Nesmith, was of great help to us in giving us insight into the spirit world. Sam says there are certain conditions which, when they exist, can serve to attract spirits if they are around. A warm, humid night, when the moon is full, is an especially logical time for them to make their presence known. The anniversary of an event, especially the death of the mortal being of the spirit, often calls them back. Put together a warm, humid, full-mooned night, and a coinciding anniversary date, and you really have a "haunting waiting to happen."

When spirits get to be too frightening or irritating and the hauntings too frequent, sometimes a gifted medium can contact the spirit, or a priest or minister can be called upon to exorcise the spirit in extreme cases. Usually just a blessing by a priest or minister will help to send the spirits towards "the light" where eternal rest and peace await them. This often helps the living residents of a house to get their own earthly rest as well!

The House on Holbrook Road

On the north side of San Antonio a quiet lane just off Eisenhauer Road follows the banks of the Salado Creek. It is called Holbrook Road. Now, this is ancient land ... land that has known both turbulence and terror, peace and plenty. According to local archaeologists, the Salado Creek site was utilized over a long period of time during the archaic era of 5500 B.C. to A.D. 1000 by Native Americans. Even now, people living in the vicinity find arrowheads, spearheads, projectile points, and various tools used by ancient man along the creek banks and adjacent acreage. It is one of the few areas in the drainage area of the Salado at which prehistoric cultural activities can still be studied in a scientific manner.

During the uneasy times that followed the Texas War for Independence in 1836, another less bloody war with Mexico took place. There was a second invasion by the Mexican army in 1842. On September 11 of that year, General Adrian Woll, a French general serving Mexico as a hired commander, marched with over 1,000 Mexican soldiers and

captured San Antonio. Soon after the news reached the city of Gonzales, over 200 volunteers under Matthew Caldwell gathered and marched to Salado Creek, about six miles east of San Antonio. On September 18 Caldwell sent John C. Hays of Texas Ranger fame with a company of men to lure the enemy out of the Alamo where they had become entrenched. The Mexicans took chase after Hays' men, who retreated to a protected site on the Salado where Caldwell and the rest of the Texans were waiting.

The engagement took place September 19, with the enemy sustaining losses of sixty dead and about as many wounded, while the Texans lost only one man killed and nine men were injured. This battle took place on and around the grounds of a house that today stands atop a grassy natural knoll on Holbrook Road. A historic marker is located there, stating that most of the battle took place between the hours of 1:45 and 2:30 p.m. on that September day. Just beyond the marker are the entry gates to the house which is now known as Victoria's Black Swan Inn.

Now, it wasn't always called the Black Swan. The beautiful white stately mansion has had a lot of names and a lot of owners and occupants. It also has been the habitat of some pretty interesting "residents" who don't seem in any hurry to go away. This brings us to the real reason for telling the story of this great white house on the hilltop.

Heinrich Mahler and his wife, Marie Biermann Mahler, immigrated to America from Germany in 1870, soon after their marriage. They wound up in Texas and, according to deed records in the Bexar County Courthouse, they purchased 200 acres of land on the east bank of Salado Creek, at what is now the corner of Rittiman and Holbrook roads, on January 14, 1887, for the sum of $2,200. Here the Mahlers built their first house overlooking the creek.

In 1897 Mahler extended his holdings by purchasing 240 acres which adjoined his property to the north for $4,556.20. After buying this second acreage, the Mahlers built a new house and moved there in 1901. This was a gracious one-story farmhouse atop a high natural knoll, overlooking the creek. Heinrich, or "Henry" as he was known locally, had farming and ranching interests and also grew cotton. His main business was dairy farming, and he sold his famous Jersey Creamery Butter for many years. The dairy barn, water tank, windmill, and stables are still located on the grounds. The Mahlers had four children: Sam, Daniel, Louise, and Sarah.

Marie Mahler died in 1923 at age 73, and Heinrich was 83 when he passed away in 1925. Both are buried in the St. John's Lutheran Cemetery.

According to a family history compiled by a great granddaughter, Pauline Gueldner Pratt, Heinrich left the house and farm to his two sons, Sam and Daniel, while the two daughters received two houses the Mahlers owned in San Antonio. Dan's portion of the inherited property consisted of the house, silo, and milk barn. Sam was given the "corner property." During the mid-1930s the Mahler farms were sold. Sam's property was purchased by Paul F. Gueldner, father-in-law of Sophie Mahler Gueldner, and was later again resold. Dan's property was purchased by two families from Wichita Falls, the Woods and the Holbrooks.

Mrs. John (nee Katherine Joline) Holbrook and Mrs. Claude (nee Blanche Joline) Woods were sisters. They and their husbands were visiting from Wichita Falls when they found and fell in love with the Mahler property and decided to purchase it. Much remodeling and enlargement took place, since the two families both planned to reside in the house and they wanted a house which would afford privacy to each family. The main body of the Mahler house was made into one extremely large drawing room, which looked out onto the long front porch. Several walls which had divided up smaller rooms had to be knocked out. Two long wings were added to either side of the center section, each wing having one very large, and one slightly smaller, bedroom, and each wing had a large bathroom and numerous closets as well.

A kitchen and dining room were to the rear of the main section of the house. There were lovely white gables on the front of the house and the new owners chose to call their home, White Gables. Except for the wings, the house still generally carried all the characteristics of the original Mahler house of 1901.

Mr. and Mrs. Holbrook had no children. The Woods had one daughter, Joline. She had been given her mother's maiden surname, since there were no boys to carry on the family name. Joline Woods lived there in the house with her parents and her aunt and uncle for a number of years until she married. Her husband was a local man, Hall Park Street, Jr. Street was born in San Antonio in 1909. He attended Washington and Lee University and was graduated with a law degree from the University of Oklahoma in 1932. He became the city's leading condemnation attorney for property owners for many years and was both a colorful and successful attorney. The Streets were very prominent in local society. Park Street served as President of the San Antonio Bar Association, President of the Order of the Alamo in 1940, and was a member of the San Antonio Country Club and the Texas Cavaliers. In 1948 he was selected as King Antonio XXVI for the Fiesta Activities that year. In other words, the Streets "belonged."

After Mr. and Mrs. Holbrook and Mr. Woods had passed away, Mrs. Woods remained in White Gables. In order that she not be alone in the big old house, Joline and Park Street and their children, Hall Park Street III and Joline, moved into the house. At this time, they added a second story which included several big bedrooms and bathrooms. The home had expanded to 16 rooms and had approximately 6,000 square feet of living space.

The socially prominent Streets entertained quite a lot in the spacious home. Among other notable guests were Mr. Street's good friends, Earle Stanley Gardner and Raymond Burr. Gardner had dedicated his "Perry Mason" series to his good friend, Park Street. Gardner was also an attorney, but his accomplishments as a writer were better known. Street was a member and one of the founders of the "Court of Last Resort." He investigated a number of cases for that court, of which Gardner was the prime founder.

In 1959 Street held formal dedication ceremonies for his Perry Mason room at his offices. He flew in the whole cast of the popular television show: Raymond Burr, Barbara Hale, William Hopper, William Tallman, Ray Collins, and of course, Earle Stanley Gardner, to help him celebrate. It is said that Gardner conceived several manuscripts for the mystery series while he was a houseguest of the Streets in their spacious home on the hill.

Joline Street died of cancer when she was rather young, in her late thirties. Her grandson, James Patrick Robinson III, was kind enough to give us a little family information. He said his grandmother died when his mother was only nineteen years old. Grandmother had been a beautiful woman, slender and fair, with dark, long hair. James said Mrs. Woods, Joline

Street's mother, had also been quite a beauty in her day, "one of the prettiest ladies in North Texas," so feminine pulchritude ran in the family.

Mrs. Woods continued to live in the house after the death of her beautiful daughter, with her son-in-law and grandchildren. Park Street finally remarried and he and his new wife evidently lived most of the time thereafter at her home on Northridge Drive. In fact, it was there that Park Street was found dead on August 4, 1965, an apparent suicide according to the *Express News* of August 6. He was found, by his wife, strangled, a belt looped around his neck and a bedpost. He had been depressed for some time according to the article, and had recently undergone psychiatric treatment in Galveston. Street died at age 55, thus bringing to an end a successful and flamboyant career.

After Park Street's death, his daughter, Joline Wood Street Robinson, and her family moved into the house with her grandmother. They remained there until she passed away, and then finally, in 1973, the house was sold to Mrs. Ingeborg Mehren.

Mrs. Mehren spent a lot of time totally refurbishing and restoring the house, clearing out the attics and storerooms, and making the house ready to become the Mehren House. The old landmark soon became known as the in place to hold receptions, luncheons, dinners, conferences, and various social events. The floor plan with its tremendous central drawing room, elegant fireplace, huge kitchen facilities (which were added onto by Mrs. Mehren), and spacious side rooms lent itself well to such activities.

Ingeborg Mehren is a most attractive lady, a native of Germany. Her husband, Dr. George Mehren, was a former diplomat. She lent a great deal of European sophistication and flair to the parties she catered at the mansion. Finally, she decided to sell the property and take on other endeavors in 1984.

The house has changed hands a couple of times since. Today it is known as Victoria's Black Swan Inn and caters largely to lavish wedding receptions. The latest owner, Jo Ann Andrews, was very gracious to receive us and show us about. We were already familiar with the house and grounds from its Mehren House years, but it was nice to revisit it and to see how it has fared under new ownership.

According to Mrs. Andrews, some very unusual "activities" have taken place at the house since her arrival on the scene. She told us that in April of 1991 she was awakened at exactly 3 a.m. for about ten nights straight. Her bedroom door would unlock, and the lights in the hallway outside would switch on, and she would open her eyes to see a man, dressed in a white shirt and dark trousers, hands on his hips, standing at the foot of her bed. She never was able to get a good look at his face, and the apparition would disappear almost immediately as soon as she saw it. She was disturbed, to say the least! She finally repositioned her bed in the room, moving it to the other side, and since then the figure has not appeared, much to her relief.

Meredith Andrews, Jo Ann's pretty young teenaged daughter, told us that on several nights, usually when it would be raining outside, she had awakened to find a man, old and wrinkled, "evil-looking," peering in her upstairs bedroom window. There is no way a human being could climb up that steeply pitched roof to such a vantage point!

Evidently, there are numerous cold spots in the house, too. Many doors will not remain locked, while others, especially the bathroom doors, will lock themselves from the outside, of their own accord. Lights often come on, especially in the south wing where Mrs. Andrews says she always feels a little uneasy. There is a large closet in the largest of the rooms, the one on the end of the wing, and she does not like to enter that space. She says the hair stands up on her arms when she opens the door, and she feels like "something" is watching her.

A recent George Strait special was partially filmed at the house and during the filming, all the lights in the south wing mysteriously came on without anyone's flipping the switches.

Mrs. Andrews says the house makes strange noises at night, and men, more than women, seem to feel uncomfortable there. She added that teenagers seem to be especially uneasy in the house at night.

There is a grand piano in the drawing room. Mrs. Andrews heard it being played one night, so she turned on the lights and ran downstairs to see what was going on. As she came into the room, the music stopped, and of course, no one was there. She also has heard the sounds of a tinkling music box, just "coming out of the walls." Her brother, who lives in a cottage on the grounds, was upstairs in the main house alone one recent afternoon, and he heard the distinct sounds of hammering downstairs. When he checked, no one was there and the hammering ceased.

For a time, the room Mrs. Andrews now uses as an office was a gift shop she ran in conjunction with the inn. There were many dolls there. She said several times when she came down in the morning, the dolls would be rearranged and the doll buggy out of place, as if some little girl had been playing dolls in the room. For this reason, Mrs. Andrews thinks maybe one of the resident spirits may be a child-spirit. There is a beautiful old doll house, or playhouse, back of the house on the grounds, which the Streets built for their daughter, Joline, when she was small.

Mrs. Andrews told us that soon after she purchased the house, she had a most unusual visitor. A woman from Dallas, accompanied by another woman and two small children, appeared at the house one day. The Dallas woman said she just wanted to look around, and then went on to explain that she had visited the place when she was a child. This must have been sometime in the mid-seventies, after Mrs. Mehren purchased the house, but before all the refurbishing had been done, which took several years, as the woman said the house was then vacant. She said at that time there were several "hippie types" that sort of hung around the place, but they didn't bother her. She said she liked to go up into the attic area where there were trunks of old clothes and dolls to play with. She also said she remembered a music box among all the belongings the previous owners had left behind. Then, she told Mrs. Andrews she really enjoyed "all the people" who would come and visit her up there in the attic! She said she had lived in an adjacent neighborhood, but did not say if she came with other playmates, or always alone. She went on to tell Mrs. Andrews she had been having disturbing dreams about the house lately and just felt compelled to come back and see it again. Mrs. Andrews has not seen the woman since that day, but she said something about her visit gave her the "creeps."

When we talked over the telephone with Mr. Henry Mahler, the only surviving grandson of the original builders, he had no ghost stories to tell, in spite of the fact the house was constructed on the site of a famous battle. Nothing disturbing ever occurred there during the time he and his parents resided in the original portion of the house. He had evidently carried on the family dairy tradition, and he did say he could recall "milking around 100 cows every day." He said the only uneasy times the family ever had was when bands of gypsies would camp across the road from the house on the creek banks. The Mahlers didn't much care to have them around, he said.

We wondered if Mrs. Andrews' occupancy had brought out the restive spirits, or if they had been about during previous ownerships. James Patrick Robinson III, the Street's grandson, had volunteered that he had felt cold spots and heard noises in the house while he had lived there with his parents and grandmother. We decided to call on Ingeborg Mehren to see if she had had any unusual experiences in the house during the days it was known as the Mehren House. Well, she certainly had, and she was kind enough to tell us about them.

As an avid student of history, Ingeborg Mehren was fascinated by the house, which she said had a certain "aura of romance and mystery." She dreamed of turning the charming old mansion into a sort of "exhibition house" . . . a combination museum and tearoom, which would reflect its gracious years of occupancy. Along with the house, she came into the possession of countless boxes, cartons, trunks, and crates of old papers, newspaper clippings, photographs, and various memorabilia that, for some reason, the former owners did not wish to take with them. She went through everything very painstakingly and had finally sorted out some fascinating mementos of the houses' history, when vandals broke into the place one night, carted off many of the most treasured items, and scattered other bits and pieces all over the property. She was absolutely devastated by this occurrence.

Mrs. Mehren was also embroiled in trying to get the city to render a permit to use the house for commercial purposes. This process stretched on for months and months. Countless trips were also made to the State Capitol in Austin to try to have the place declared a historical landmark. It was through Mrs. Mehren's efforts that the historical marker near the front gates was finally placed.

After the act of vandalism took place, Mrs. Mehren realized there was need for a resident caretaker to stay in the house and deter any further acts of vandalism, while she was sorting and cataloging all the belongings. The first "house sitters" were a young couple who worked part-time and attended a local college as well.

Now, Ingeborg Mehren had been told by several local residents that she had purchased what was purported to be a haunted house, but not believing in such things, she took little notice. However, she did wonder when the young woman who had taken up residence there told her that there was "a lady . . . a beautiful lady, like a special presence," upstairs in the largest bedroom. She described her as young and lovely, and she was wearing a sort of "headband . . . like in the flapper days. It had a jeweled motif in the center over her forehead and a little feather to the back." She told Ingeborg that she felt the woman, who had appeared several times, was friendly and did not mind them being there. Ingeborg thought the young woman was really seeing things!

Then, several days later, as she was going through a box of assorted newspaper clippings, she stumbled across one that announced that Joline Woods, a local debutante, had been selected to travel to Washington, D.C. to represent San Antonio at a gala ball. The accompanying photograph showed her to be a beautiful young woman, and she was wearing a headband, complete with jeweled center and a jaunty feather in the back! Ingeborg said she started to believe . . . .

When the summer ended, the young couple moved out, and Mehren next hired an elderly Mexican man, who was a bit hard of hearing, to move in and take care of things. Several days after he took up residence, she called on him to see how he was getting along. He had moved his mattress and bedding to the back porch of the house. She asked him why he wasn't staying in the bedroom she had arranged for him. He told her, "Oh, no, senora, hay muchos santos en la casa" ("no ma'm . . . there are many spirits in the house"). He then also told her that there was a lot of noise and music that disturbed him. The spirits must have been equipped with stereophonic sound, as the poor man was nearly deaf!

Then there was a brief stay by a retired military couple, and several other temporary caretakers, who came . . . and who went . . . .

For a short time, Ingeborg had a very distinguished guest who consented to stay at the house during an extended visit to San Antonio. He was Franz Wilhelm, Prince of Prussia. One time when he was entertaining a visitor from Austria, also of noble birth, the two men saw a man appear at the upstairs window five or six times during the course of the evening. He was elderly with a "menacing expression," they said. The Austrian, who said he was somewhat psychic, told the prince that he felt the man was evil and was connected to a murder. When Ingeborg heard this she said for the first time she felt very uncomfortable in the house.

Ingeborg said she often felt the presence of a woman in the house, especially in the largest upstairs bedroom to the left of the stairs. She said she got to where she would talk to the spirit, saying, "I hope you are happy that we are having such nice parties here." She felt a friendly benevolence in that room as if her messages had indeed reached the spirit.

Christa Rabaste, Ingeborg's secretary, had an office adjacent to Ingeborg's. They would always lock up when they left in the evening, but at times, when arriving in the morning, they would find the house unlocked and all the lights turned on! Often Mrs. Rabaste would find desk drawers open, the closet door ajar, and things in general disarray, on a fairly regular basis. However, neither she nor Ingeborg Mehren ever found anything missing.

Several waiters who worked at the house after it had finally been converted to a party house told Mrs. Mehren they didn't like to be in the house alone at night when they were cleaning up after a party. They said they would hear a music box playing, and the sounds would follow them all around the house. Mrs. Mehren said she had also heard both the music box and hammering noises, although she could never locate the sources. An elderly Mexican lady who cleaned there told her she liked to work there because there was "such nice music in the house."

Ingeborg said just "lots of things happened . . . it would take too long to tell everything," but she made it clear that she had certainly changed from the nonbeliever in ghosts she was when she first purchased the house. In fact, she finally had asked a friend, who was a Catholic priest, if he would come and give Mehren House a "blessing." This was not an exorcism, but she said she felt more comfortable after the priest had made his visit. She recalled one strange thing that happened while he made his rounds of the house. When he got to the top of the stairs and headed to the bedroom on the left, where the young woman in the headband had appeared to the housesitter, and where Ingeborg often had felt a "presence," he told her,

"For some reason I think I'd better give this room a double blessing!"

After hearing about so many manifestations from both Jo Ann Andrews and Ingeborg Mehren, we decided to ask our friend, Sam Nesmith, a well-known historian and also a psychic, if he would consent to visit the Black Swan Inn with us. At his request, we told him nothing we had heard from either the former or current owner. All he knew was that the place was supposed to be haunted. We drove to the house one sunny afternoon and let Sam wander, at will, about the house and grounds to see what kind of vibrations he might be able to pick up.

Just before we reached the gates which open up on the long driveway approach to the house, Sam picked up on something. He said it was rather "unsettling." As we drove on up the driveway, he said he felt some "tumult" there. Of course, this is where the Battle of Salado Creek had taken place!

Mrs. Andrews invited us in, and we walked with Sam, slowly, all over the house and grounds. He said in the house he felt no violence, but he did feel it on the grounds. As we walked over the large mansion, Sam would sometimes pause as he "felt something" somewhere. The south wing brought forth a comment that there was definitely "something" about the closet Mrs. Andrews had mentioned that she did not like to open. He said the hair stood up on his arms as he thrust them inside the opening. He felt someone might have had a safe or cabinet for valuables there at one time, and was still zealously guarding them. In the middle of the wing there is a small bedroom where he said he felt someone, most likely a woman, had been very ill and confined to bed for a long time. There was a certain "sadness" in the room, but no indication that a death had occurred there. (Our visit with Ingeborg Mehren had included her telling us that Mrs. Woods was very frail and confined to her room for some time before her granddaughter had had to place her in a nursing home. This was apparently the room she had occupied. Ingeborg told us a maid who had worked there had told her that Mrs. Woods was very sad when she realized she was going to have to leave her beloved home.)

Sam was not very comfortable on the steep stairs leading to the second floor. He said he felt something rather ominous in that area, and in the area just below the trap door leading up to the attic, which Mrs. Andrews has had nailed down, so

101

that it is pretty much inaccessible now. As he walked up the stairs, Sam said he "saw" a large gilt mirror on the wall at the head of the stairs. There is no mirror hanging there now, but Mrs. Mehren later told us that there had been one there all the time she had the house!

In the bedroom where Mrs. Andrews had experienced her mysterious nocturnal visitor, Sam felt no sense of danger or anxiety, but he did pick up on certain "energies."

To the left of the top of the stairs is the largest bedroom with a dressing room, which faces the rear yard of the house. This is where the house-sitter had seen the young woman in the headband . . . and the same room Ingeborg had felt a certain presence. The dressing area is completely covered with mirrors and a lot of built-in cabinetry. Here, Sam strongly felt a "definite presence of a woman . . . she is a beautiful woman, sort of a Yvonne deCarlo type, long, dark hair, lovely fair skin, very sophisticated and vibrant. She died fairly young, but she is very possessive of this area," Sam concluded. He went on to say she liked to be "in charge of things" and feels it is still her house, but she is not a threatening presence. He did say it would not surprise him if she made a "real physical appearance" in that room one of these days, as the energy was so strong there.

We went back downstairs. Sam strolled into the kitchen area. This was the old kitchen area that belonged to the original Mahler house, not the long addition added during the Mehren House era. Here he instantly picked up on another spirit. This one was also a woman, but a "very different type. She is rather short and stout, in her late sixties or early seventies, with her gray hair pulled back into a knot at the back of her head. She is very busy here, either kneading bread or making biscuits or something . . . she is very contented here," he concluded. In fact, he added she is a sort of "guardian spirit." Later, when Mrs. Andrews showed Sam a picture of the elderly Mrs. Mahler, he said she looked just like the woman he had seen in the kitchen!

And, of course, after hearing Sam's description of the beautiful spirit upstairs, we found it to perfectly fit the description of Joline Woods Street that her grandson, James Patrick Robinson III, had given us. Sam was doing alright!

The glassed-in porch, now used as a bar area, was one place where Sam felt some sort of "dominant spirit" . . . a very dynamic sort of male spirit. Sam said he felt the man was probably a "large, dark haired middle-aged man" . . . also very possessive of the house, but not a violent presence. Of course, Park Street was a large, middle-aged and dark-haired man, and from all accounts a very strong personality as well.

From the stories we heard from Mrs. Andrews and Mrs. Mehren, and from Sam's comments, we have come to the conclusion that Victoria's Black Swan Inn, formerly the Mehren House, formerly White Gables, formerly the Mahler homestead, definitely has "resident spirits," and they will probably continue to remain there. We believe Mrs. Mahler is happy in her kitchen, beautiful Joline Woods Street is ensconced in her bedroom-dressing room area, and that the sounds of the music box and the piano will continue to be heard. We don't know who the man is who appeared in the night to Jo Ann Andrews, nor who the old man at the upstairs window might be. Sam says there is nothing to fear in the house, but there are definitely "star boarders" at Victoria's Black Swan Inn!

The Wolfson Manor

In downtown San Antonio, at 415 South Broadway, directly across the street from the San Antonio Light Building, stands a charming old Victorian house . . . the last of the River Road mansions of the late 1800s.

Today the house of over 5,042 square feet is crowded between business establishments, but once it had a large front and back yard. In fact, the grounds to the rear of the house once extended back to the San Antonio River, some distance away.

From an article in the 1981 edition of *San Antonio Monthly Magazine*, and "A History of First Baptist San Antonio's Wolfson House" which is provided to visitors to the house, we gathered a wealth of intriguing information. We are also indebted to Mr. Chester Webb, a former owner, and Mrs. Frieda Reed, who, with her husband, Warren, rented the house at one time, for additional information. You see, in addition to being

a beautiful example of Victorian architecture, the house is reputed to be occupied at times by other-worldly visitors!

The stone dwelling, with upper and lower front porches and an attractive bay window, was built in 1888-89 by a Prussian-born merchant, Mr. Saul Wolfson. He operated the Wolfson Dry Goods Store on Main Plaza, across Dolorosa Street from the San Fernando Cathedral. He no doubt enjoyed a daily carriage ride from his home on Broadway to the location of his store. The business must have been very successful, as the house he provided for his wife, Emelia, and their four sons was beautifully equipped with eight fireplaces, lovely hardwood floors, rolled window glass, and fourteen foot ceilings. In addition, there were colorless art glass panes in the front door, which are thought to be Lalique. A beautiful Tiffany glass panel adorned the stairwell, and stained glass panes fitted into the transoms. Beautiful brass gaslight fixtures illuminated the house.

In his later years, Mr. Wolfson moved his offices to his residence. Here he kept his files, his personal library, and a huge walk-in safe. Later on, we were fascinated to learn, the safe became a bathroom shower!

Saul Wolfson died on December 16, 1923. He left his estate to his widow, Emelia, and his four sons, Abe, Emil, Milton, and Jesse.

Abe Wolfson, a bachelor who survived his mother and his siblings, stayed in the family abode for many years before he sold it in 1967 to Mr. and Mrs. Chester Webb. Mr. Webb told us that Abe had lived mainly in just one room, choosing to run extension cords all over the house. Unlike many old houses that were later chopped up and made into boarding houses or apartments, the Wolfson house had been kept intact, and "except for lots of dust," Mr. Webb said the place was in good condition.

The Webbs renovated the house and used it as both a residence and an art gallery. Mr. Webb said the house had been almost hidden from view by trees, overgrown bushes, and weeds at the time they purchased it with many of its original furnishings. A rickety double-decker porch in back was replaced by ground level decking, window-unit air conditioners were installed to heat and cool the rooms, and a new roof was added. New plumbing fixtures also were installed. Mr. Webb noted that although it was no longer used, an old brick outhouse, a "two holer," which had at some time had a modern commode seat added on one side, was left intact in the back of the house.

At the time the Webbs renovated the house, a lot of interesting items were found throughout the house, which had a lot of hidden nooks and crannies. Some of these revealed the hiding places for all sorts of things. Hidden behind a wall in the old dining room was a box that was labeled "Wash Woman." When opened, a place setting for eight of lovely silver was discovered . . . quite a valuable surprise!

Another Wolfson family memento was also discovered . . . a little embossed silver box with a bit of paper tightly rolled up inside. The message written on the paper said, "Darling, would you please put your rings in this little box instead of on the floor?"

According to the Baptist leaflet on the house, Mrs. Miller (formerly Mrs. Webb) said the gentle ghost of Emelia Wolfson still visits her beloved old home. Once a portrait of Mrs. Wolfson was removed from a parlor wall and placed behind a door. Evidentially Emelia didn't appreciate being tucked away out of sight, because after a long night filled with slamming doors and mysterious footsteps, the picture was found the next morning, hanging in its usual spot. Unless displayed in a prominent place, the portrait would not stay put. It would just move itself! Mrs. Miller is quoted as saying that she had seen the ghost . . . "a small, gray haired woman, who moved through the downstairs rooms, as illusive as smoke."

According to the *San Antonio Monthly* article, "An after hours employee was said to have once become aware of a presence in the room with her. Turning, she saw the shadowy outlines of a diminutive woman watching her every move. Uttering not a sound, the ethereal sprite moved silently from the room, the vague outlines of her form disappearing before she reached the door, but not before the employee could distinguish the ghost as the same woman whose portrait graced the walls of Wolfson Manor."

Mrs. Miller said she and two friends once watched a large curio cabinet levitate and settle without its contents being a bit disturbed!

Over the years the house has changed ownership several times and has been rented out as well. In 1979 Mr. Warren Reed leased the house and for about four years maintained his advertising business at the locale. We talked to Mrs. Frieda Reed, and she said they enjoyed the lovely building and its gracious atmosphere, which was very conducive to the creativity required in the advertising profession. However, she said a few strange things did happen during the time her husband maintained his business there. She did say she didn't really believe in ghosts, however . . . .

One night, while there in the house alone in the upstairs rooms, Mr. Reed heard a door open downstairs, and then he distinctly heard footsteps moving around. A check downstairs revealed all the doors to be locked, and no one was about. Then, a young woman who worked in the photography darkroom said she swore she had seen a "little old lady" appear to her. And once, Mrs. Reed stated, when her son and some of his young friends were upstairs in the old house at night, they heard the footsteps of what they supposed was an intruder walking around in the lower part of the house. They all grabbed some heavy metal T-squares and dashed downstairs, prepared to encounter a burglar. There was no one to be found, and again, all the doors were locked!

In 1982 the First Baptist San Antonio purchased the house from the Spires Douglas Corporation. They have attractively restored the building and it is now used by the church for Sunday School activities, class functions, receptions and parties, and arts and crafts events. A large wrought iron fence surrounds the property and a historical plaque can be seen on the wall beside the front door. Evidentially, there have been no recent visits by Mrs. Wolfson to her old homestead. Maybe there's just too much activity going on these days, and she's located some more tranquil surroundings!

Miss Ernestine's Adobe Dwelling

Just a stone's throw across the San Antonio River from the grounds of the Lone Star Brewery, at the confluence of Mission Road and Yellowstone Street, stands a little mill house with a water wheel by the side of the road. Behind the mill house there's an old adobe house that can just barely be glimpsed through the shrubs and trees. This historic landmark home, known as the Yturri-Edmunds Home is now a property of the San Antonio Conservation Society.

The house has a fascinating history! The property on which it is located was once part of the fields belonging to nearby Mission Concepcion. Manuel Yturri-Castillo secured a land grant for the property from the Mexican government in 1824 and soon constructed a three-room adobe house. The bricks were a combination of earth (probably clay from the banks of a nearby river), goat's hair, and goat's milk. The walls constructed of the material were over eighteen inches thick.

After Manuel died, the house was left to his daughter, Vicenta. By then there was a small house, a mill, and a bar on the property. Vicenta married an Anglo settler named Ernest Edmunds, and they soon added three more rooms onto the little house and began to rear a family. Ernest, who was not a

very astute businessman, died young, at age thirty-four. In fact, he died on the very day in August 1874 that his youngest daughter, Ernestine, was born. Vicenta was left with a new baby and two other small children, Josephine and Edgar. The death of her husband left the young widow in financial need, so she used her fluency in English, Spanish, and French to gain a position as a schoolteacher at Mission Concepcion. She also held classes for neighboring children from ages ten through fifteen in her home, where she taught reading, writing, religion, and health.

The three children grew up in the little adobe house under their mother's tutelage. Ernestine was especially scholarly, and longed to follow in her mother's footsteps. When she was only sixteen years of age, she began to teach at Harlandale's Old Morrill Chapel School. Later on, during the teaching career that was to span fifty years, she also taught at the Alamo Heights Elementary School, often riding horseback clear across town to teach her classes. "Miss Ernestine" never married, and she chose to live out her life right under the same roof where she had been born. She lived with her mother, Vicenta, and her spinster sister, Josephine, until their deaths in 1924. Ernestine continued living in the house until she passed away in 1961 at the age of eighty-seven.

After she retired from teaching, "Miss Ernestine" dreamed of making a little museum of her adobe home. She also thought of making a classroom or art studio of the old mill house so children could come there to study. Sidney Yarbrough, a member of the Conservation Society and Chairman of the Yturri-Edmunds House and grounds told us that "children were Miss Ernestine's life."

Ernestine had a very limited income and was never able to achieve her wish of making her house into a museum. As she left no heirs, she chose to will her property to the San Antonio Conservation Society in 1961, doubtless knowing by doing so, it would be preserved.

Back of the house and next to the little mill house, there is a charming little rock grotto that Ernestine built from honeycomb rocks she'd collected over the years. There is a lovely statue of the Virgin in the grotto, and an inscription that reads, "At this spot on several occasions appeared a vision of a lady in white to my mother, Vicenta Edmunds."

It seems that both Ernestine's sister, Josephine, and her mother, Vicenta, had reported seeing a "vision" there shortly before they died. Both ladies were ill and close to death at the time the visions appeared. When Ernestine later questioned her priest about the visions, he explained that since both ladies were approaching death, he felt the spirit of the Blessed Mother had appeared to put them at ease, so they would not be afraid to die. Josephine had also seen a beautiful white bird with long tail feathers up in a tree. The priest believed the Virgin had appeared in this guise to Josephine to show her presence to her prior to her death. The mother, Vicenta, had seen the figure of a woman dressed in white shortly before she died. Although Ernestine never saw one of these visions, she believed her mother and sister had, and that is why she constructed the grotto.

Mrs. Yarbrough and several docents who take tour groups through the house all feel there is definitely a guardian spirit at the place. It could be any of the women who lived there so long . . . Ernestine, Josephine, or their mother, Vicenta. Or, maybe all three of them come back at one time or another . . . who can tell? Many Conservation Society members who are regular visitors to the house have reported feeling a presence in the house . . . others experience cold spots and are quite uncomfortable there. One member, Minnie Campbell, said she feels very "ill at ease" when she is there. Mrs. Yarbrough says there's at least one member who won't go in the adobe house at all . . . "she gets a bad feeling when she is there, and it makes her unhappy and frightened."

A young man with whom I spoke, Lawrence Hill, who has served as a docent for several months this summer, said he had recently talked with a woman who stated she was frightened to enter the house. He said he himself had had at least one day when he felt "very uncomfortable, sort of depressed" and he had felt a definite presence that day. He had caught a fleeting glimpse . . . of someone or something, flitting by his peripheral line of vision . . . but when he searched about, he could find no one there.

Mrs. Yarbrough thinks there really could be a ghost there . . . or it could just be a strong energy . . . a "strong love," because so many of Miss Ernestine's possessions are in the house, you can't help but feel her presence. For instance, there's an old clock from the E. N. Welch Manufacturing Company. The clock stopped on the day that Vicenta Edmunds died. Miss Ernestine had written on a little piece of paper, "Mother loved her old clock, but it was stopped on the day of her death." It was signed, "Josephine and Ernestine." The date written on the paper was June 6, 1924, Friday, 2:45 a.m.

Edgar, the only boy in the family, had married and left the homestead. However, the marriage did not work out. On the day he died, he had taken his wife to a lawyer to sign over some insurance papers to her prior to the divorce. He then took a bus (no one in the Edmunds family ever had a car) and headed to his sister's home. Somewhere, in the short block between Roosevelt Street, where he got off the bus, and the little house a block down on Yellowstone, he was mysteriously shot and killed. No killer was ever brought to justice.

Mrs. Yarbrough doesn't believe anyone was really unhappy in the house. But because they lived there so long . . . all their lives, in fact, the spirits of the ladies just must have a hard time giving up the old home they loved to strangers.

We feel sure Miss Ernestine would be flattered and happy to know that each year, on the anniversary of her birthday, the members of the Conservation Society gather at the house for a special party to commemorate her birthday, honoring her for her long service to the community.

A Warm and Welcoming Presence

The lovely old Sartor House at 217 King William Street is owned by a charming lady, Mrs. A. R. (Julia) Cauthorn, who has resided in the city for many years. The delightful house was built around 1882 by Alexander Sartor, who came to San Antonio as a German immigrant.

Alfred Giles, the famous English architect who designed many notable buildings in the area, was the architect for Mr. Sartor, who owned one of San Antonio's first jewelry stores, and was also well known as an expert watch repairman.

Mr. Sartor lived in the house until his retirement in 1909. Sartor passed away in 1915.

In the 1960s the house was owned by the Tobin Foundation and was once used for a time by the Family Welfare Association. Later it served as a guest house for visitors to the 1968 Hemisfair. Mrs. Cauthorn purchased the house in 1972 and substantially restored it.

The one-story dwelling is unique in that it has caliche block construction on a limestone foundation. Its long front porch presents a welcoming effect to the passer-by, with an

Italianate Victorian facade, boasting stately columns and a raised archway over the front entrance. The trim, in the original colors, is in dark and golden brown tones. Louvered shutters accent the four long front windows which reach from floor to ceiling, affording a maximum breeze on hot summer evenings. Like so many of the old homes in the King William area, the ceiling of the porch is painted pale sky blue. The German settlers there believed wasps would not nest in a blue ceiling, as they would think it was the sky!

A magnificent magnolia tree shades the front yard and a delicate wrought iron picket fence separates the yard from the front sidewalk.

Mrs. Cauthorn said when she moved in, she had never slept in a house alone. The first night she slept in one of the side parlors, as the bedrooms were not yet ready for occupancy. As she lay in bed on that first evening, she was quite exhausted from the exertion of moving. She thought, "should I be afraid, here all alone in this old house?" She said she then had the strangest feeling, as if a presence unseen, yet keenly felt, had moved from the parlor across the central hallway, into the room where she lay. It seemed to reach out to her as if to say "Welcome! Don't be afraid." She felt so comforted that she soon fell into a deep sleep.

Sometime in the night she awoke to the sound of rain falling on the old tin roof, and again she thought, "I'm all alone in this house." This time, she again felt this unbelievably warm, welcoming presence surrounding her. She said the only way she could describe it was to say she felt warm and protected as if someone had wrapped loving arms around her to assure her all would be well.

A short time later, a friend from Austin, who had referred to Julia's new purchase as "Julia's folly," arrived for a visit. She said the very first thing she felt as she entered the house was a feeling of such warmth and welcome it was hard to describe . . . she just had to eat her words about "Julia's folly."

Julia said as a child she had once visited the house for a concert of chamber music. Her godmother had taken her there when she was only about six years old. Although that was many years ago, she still vividly recalls her first introduction to the heavenly strains of the harp and violin. Now, occasionally, she hosts chamber musicales in her lovely home!

Julia Cauthorn maintains the house has brought her, and her many visitors, such joy and warmth, she refers to it as her "Magic House." Although the protective spirit has not again presented itself as tangibly as it did on her first night of residency, it is doubtless still there, watching over its old home and the loving owner who continues to preserve and cherish it.

A Sickeningly Sweet Smell

Laura Beckley still remembers a visit she and her then-husband, Ken Williamson, made back in the early '80s to visit her mother, Vivien Beckley, who lived in the hill country north of Boerne. Mrs. Beckley's house was a sprawling five-thousand-square-foot building of cedar and rock construction. Its retaining walls and water tanks abutted the house.

Laura hadn't grown up there; her mother had only been living in the house a few years. A great place to visit, the house had several spacious guest rooms. On this particular visit, the room in which Laura usually slept had been rearranged and had just a single bed, so the Williams were given another room for this visit.

About 11:30 p.m. Laura decided to retire, leaving her husband reading and watching television. She settled down in bed and soon drifted off to sleep. Then, suddenly, she awoke! She felt a strange presence in the room. Then, there was the feeling of something coiling around her neck, and she felt she was being choked. She likened the feeling to that of having hands grasping her neck. Then, at the same time, she felt a weight pushing against her, forcing her down in the bed. And the smell! It was an aroma that could only be described as "sickly sweet" . . . so sweet it was almost painful. There was nothing floral about it. It burned her nose and was so strong in its intensity she could scarcely breathe. Laura said she had never smelled anything she could compare it with, but there was no doubt in her mind that the presence of the aroma reflected something "very evil."

Consumed with fear, Laura forced herself out of bed and ran into the room where her husband was reading. She tried to explain to him what had happened, but he didn't seem to believe her. He accompanied her back to the bedroom, but as soon as she set foot inside the room, she again detected the sickly sweet smell. She grew icy cold and shook with chills. Her husband, on the other hand, smelled nothing, nor did he feel anything unusual.

Laura said "I just couldn't go back into that room . . . every time I walked back into it the smell was still there. I stood in the hall and even with my husband there and the lights on . . . I couldn't force myself to go back in that bedroom."

Laura said when she told her mother how she felt, she understood, as she said she had had some unusual feelings, too. Laura said she didn't go back into that room again during that visit, and during subsequent visits she never slept in that room again.

A year or so later, in September of 1982, the house burned to the ground. There was no reason to suspect arson. The speculation was that squirrels had chewed up some of the wiring in the attic.

Laura's mother rebuilt the house on the old foundation, but she used a different floor plan. After that, when she went to the location of the frightening bedroom, Laura said there was no lingering sweet smell or feeling of a ghostly presence there.

Years before her mother had bought the house, there had been a Mexican family working for the previous owners, and someone told Laura's mother that one of them had been drowned in a tank on the place. Laura never believed that particular death had anything to do with the feelings she had experienced in that bedroom.

Nor does Laura believe that the "spirit" or whatever it was that generated the sweet smell and the choking sensations was the cause of the fire. She does believe that the spirit or "presence" left after the fire and has never returned. Vivien Beckley has since sold the house, and the new owners have not reported any usual experiences, substantiating Laura's belief that the spirit departed when the fire consumed the house.

The Gothic Window

When local artist Jesse Sanchez was an art major at Trinity University, he and three other students lived off campus in a two-story rock house in the Scenic Loop area of Helotes. The community is a rather plush, wooded residential area just north of San Antonio. Sanchez said in the 1950s it was cheaper to live in Helotes than rent a place around the university.

All four students had jobs, and they alternated with their household chores. On a particularly beautiful, moonlit night nearly forty years ago, Jesse recalls it was his evening to stay home.

He had decided to sort out some books. "As I sat going through my books, I chanced to look out the window, and I saw a tall, Gothic window, the medieval type, perfectly symmetrical in shape. It was taller than any of the trees surrounding the area."

Sanchez said the area was sparsely inhabited, with only one house within shouting distance. Although awed, frightened, and puzzled, he decided to go outside and try to walk towards the window. As he walked up an incline, he knew no one was about. He saw nothing but bare ground, "but that was the way it was supposed to be."

He came back inside and returned to his room. Still puzzled, he settled down to continue his work with his books. He tried to figure out an explanation for the vision, but there just wasn't any. And then he glanced out the window again, and lo and behold! there was the Gothic window again!

Even though tempted, Jesse did not go outside again. He did wish he could have found an explanation for the sudden appearance of the beautiful window. Ever the artist, he said he would have liked to have committed the scene to canvas!

The Tidy Ghost

Lillian Gonzales remembers back when she was just a little girl four or five years old, an old family friend would often visit her parents. His name was Jose Quiroz, a widower who lived alone on El Paso Street in San Antonio's southwest side. Lillian says his house, which was built in the 1920s, always seemed "different." It not only had a basement, a rare feature in San Antonio's houses, but it had an upstairs area with gabled windows. Most of the houses in the neighborhood were much smaller, and Quiroz's house seemed very affluent to his neighbors!

"Each time he'd visit us, he'd talk about his ghost," recalled Lillian. "When he spoke of the ghost, it wasn't a scary thing for me, I was so fascinated by his mysterious stories."

Quiroz told them, "Every night at about midnight, a lady, all dressed in white, with a veil covering her, came up the basement steps and moved to the backyard. It there was a breeze, she made a beautiful picture with the wind blowing her robes as she walked across the yard in the direction of the corner barbecue pit."

The old gentleman described the ghost's actions as if she were performing the chores of a cleaning woman, as she worked around and inside the barbecue pit. He described her as a very "meticulous sort of spirit" because after she was finished cleaning, she'd even get a broom and sweep until everything was in order! When the ghostly chores were done, the ethereal figure would again float to the basement stairs and disappear until time for her to come out the next night.

Lillian said she recalled as a small youngster she had a very inquisitive mind and she'd press Mr. Quiroz for more information. "Did she do the same thing every night?" to which Mr. Quiroz would reply, "Yes, yes, she came every single night." Quiroz even took the little girl over to see the basement, since she didn't know what a basement was, and pointed out this was where the ghost came from every night to do all the dusting and cleaning.

Lillian's lively imagination kept triggering more and more questions. The patient Mr. Quiroz answered her question, "who is the ghost?" by saying at first he wasn't sure who she might be, but as he watched and observed her more closely, he noticed her only concern seemed to be the rock house and yard. It became clearer to him that it must be the spirit of his first wife, Mary. He said, "I think she is still checking up on me and making sure my house is still in order."

Neighbors of Quiroz who had heard his story would come over to see him and stay past midnight, hoping to glimpse the ghost. No one but Quiroz was ever able to see her, apparently.

Later, Quiroz remarried, and the second Mrs. Quiroz was not interested in staying up late to try and get a glimpse of the spirit of her husband's first wife. If the ghost was indeed, Mary Quiroz, she must have become convinced the second marriage for her husband was happy and harmonious, because she soon ceased her nightly visits.

Maybe she just decided it was time for the new Mrs. Quiroz to take over the cleaning chores!

Ramon Ramos Has a Ghostly Housemate

When Ramon Ramos returned to live in San Antonio after many years of residing in both Chicago and New York, he decided to settle in the historic Monte Vista area. The "dream house" he purchased in 1964 is a two-story dwelling with spacious rooms and a lawn shaded by a huge century-old Spanish oak tree. The lovely home on a quiet street was just the place where the decorator and window display artist could display the antiques and memorabilia he had collected during his sixteen-year career.

Ramon enjoyed about eight years of enjoyable, tranquil living in the house, and noted nothing strange about his residence at all. Then in 1972 a friend from Germany, Claus Van der Hausen, came for a short visit. One morning when Ramon was sitting in the breakfast room his visitor informed him that the house had "a spirit."

Ramon said, "I didn't exactly understand what he meant, and I asked him if he could possible mean a ghost." He said his guest replied, "Yes, you have a nice ghost." Ramos said "I can't believe it!" Then Van der Hausen remarked, "You will, because eventually it will start talking to you."

A few months later Ramos did begin to hear footsteps in his bedroom. He said he questioned the ghost, or being, and said to it, "I don't know what you are trying to do, but you are not scaring me a bit. I want to know more about you."

Ramos continued, recalling his first conversation with the ghost, "I think the best thing is to tell you this is my house now. I love it. I will not destroy it, so feel free to roam or do whatever you want."

As the footsteps continued, Ramos went so far as to take a friend with him up into the attic to see if anything unusual was there, but they found nothing. "I even blew some insulation into the attic, but that didn't stop the footsteps," he said.

About three years after he first started hearing the footsteps, another guest, Bill Radde, stopped over for a few days. Ramon said he put him up in the master bedroom. The following morning, he too reported he had an encounter with a ghost. Radde said that the ghost came and sat on the bed and that he didn't have much room because the uninvited guest took up most of the space. He also said he felt the ghost nudging at his feet. In fact, he told Ramos he experienced the same thing a second time before he finished his visit!

Then about ten years ago, a married couple, Jerry and Dulcey Burns, visited Ramos from Illinois. Both Jerry and

Dulcey said they encountered the ghost, but they just ignored the experience.

Ramon purchased the house from Jane and Bill Blaylock. Ramos does not know if they ever had any experience with the ghost. Nor does he know who the guest ghost is. Those houseguests who have seen the ghost have told Ramon that it is a young boy, but Ramon doesn't know the age because he personally has never seen the apparition. His personal opinion is the ghostly intruder might be a former resident of the house. There have been six families in possession of the house at one time or another, he said.

Today, Ramon comfortably coexists with his ghost, who usually comes at night when it is quiet and the television and music have been turned off. He places the time sometime between eleven o'clock and midnight. "The ghost has never spoken to me," says Ramon, in spite of the prediction of his first guest. He says, "I hear only footsteps." When he hears them, Ramon just calmly says, "Now, enough is enough! I want to go to sleep!"

The Cold Parlor

As a child, Theda Sueltenfuss grew up in a one-story frame dwelling built in 1907 by her grandparents. Located in the beautiful hill country between the towns of Boerne and Comfort, the place looked very much like any other modest frame dwelling of that era, with lots of gingerbread work and a nice front porch. But Theda thinks it was "different" somehow.

There was a formal front parlor in the house that was seldom used. Theda always felt it had an "unfriendly, scary atmosphere," and as a little girl she had been afraid to go into the room, which was kept dark and closed up most of the time. In contained an eclectic array of furniture, most of which were antique pieces.

By the 1960s the "parlor look" had vanished as the room was transformed into a bedroom. Theda said it still seemed mysterious to her and she was always "afraid I would find something" when she went into the room.

Not long after the remodeling, a house guest from El Paso was assigned the newly converted bedroom. A short while after the guest retired, she came and told Theda's mother she had heard the window rattling. She was very frightened and as white as a sheet. On another occasion the same visitor told of seeing a bright light on the bedroom wall. Another guest who spent the night in the same room was very disturbed over the collection of antique dolls that Theda had placed in the bedroom. She said she couldn't stand to have the dolls "looking at her."

On still another occasion, Theda said her parents were showing their prized antiques off to a guest and when they entered the parlor-turned-bedroom the guest said "This room is cold, and the hair on my arms is standing up." Lots of other people have noted they felt a cold spot in the bedroom. Theda said a friend named Steve had once told her he had heard someone, or something, breathing heavily in the room, and he could feel a heavy pressure on his chest at the same time. He said the sounds of the breathing lasted a long while.

Years later Theda moved to Dallas. She still had strange feelings about that one room in her parents' home. When she moved back to South Texas and went to visit them, she said she would always wait outside the house for them to return rather than enter the house alone.

For years Theda said she had the feeling she might open the door to that room and a "monster" would be in that old parlor. She doesn't know why, but the feeling has continued to persist. She said to her knowledge no one had ever died or been killed in the house. So why does the old house still call up a feeling of fear and foreboding to Theda?

Was It Premonition?

Theda Sueltenfuss lives in a house near Comfort, north of San Antonio that once belonged to her Aunt Marie. She has spent much time and money restoring and redecorating the place, which she believes is still presided over by the loving spirit of her late aunt.

The hill country home was owned by Theda's mother's late brother and his wife. Her uncle died about forty years ago, and his wife passed away twenty years ago. The day before her aunt's death, Theda recalls her father drove over from his home nearby to take Marie to the grocery store in Comfort. After they returned to her house with the groceries, she invited her brother-in-law in for a cold beer and a visit. She began to tearfully reminisce, saying how much she missed her husband. In her reflective mood she also gave the elder Sueltenfuss some information he had not previously been given, such as where the key to her lock box was located, what kind of funeral she wanted, and what clothing she wanted to be buried in. He later wondered, did she have a premonition of her impending death?

Despite having had some heart trouble, that day Marie showed no signs of illness. Therefore it was a great shock to the family when hunters who were on her place the next day called to say they had found her dead.

The family immediately went to the house to carry out Marie's wishes. Nothing had been disturbed there. In fact, food was still on the table where she had apparently enjoyed her last meal.

The family members congregated in a seldom used bedroom, where Marie had kept most of her clothes. There on the bed was a little pillow, which none of them had ever seen before. Embroidered on the cover was the message, "Good Luck to You."

When they returned to the house the next day the family discovered a Christmas card in blue, with gold praying hands, on the dining room table. They had not seen it before. How strange, they thought, for a Christmas card to be there in October!

Theda said her aunt was buried, according to her wishes, in Comfort. Soon after her death, Theda began to have dreams about her aunt and the house in which she had lived. In the dreams, her aunt was walking in her yard, and she told Theda everything was all right. In one dream that Theda vividly recalls, her aunt told her she had decided to move back into her house!

The dreams continued off and on for years. Then, Theda learned from a close friend of her aunt's that her fervent wish had been for Theda to take the house, fix it up, and then move in and live there. By then, the house had been closed up for a long while, everything having been left as it had been at the time of Marie's death. Theda said, "We always had the feeling that she didn't want anything moved."

No one in the family had stayed there in the house alone since Marie had passed away. Most of the family had the feeling that "someone, or something, was watching them."

Now Theda is trying to make her aunt's wishes come true, and at the same time, she is trying to overcome the eerie feeling she has long had about being alone in the house as she goes about redecorating the old place.

Theda recently told a guest in her home about often feeling a presence in the house. A week later, her friend remarked that she had seen Marie in the house, and went on to describe her appearance perfectly, although she had never once seen her during her lifetime!

Theda is beginning to feel more at ease in the house. She believes her aunt's spirit is still there, but she is so pleased that Theda is taking such good care of things that she has become a very contented spirit. This certainly makes things a lot more "comfortable" for Theda, over there in Comfort!

The Ghost Who Liked Lavender

When an acquaintance of ours and her husband moved into a "new" old house in the historic King William District, they didn't realize it already had a "resident." The house, built in 1903, was long in the possession of an elderly widow, who lived there alone. She died several years ago of apparent natural causes, and her body was discovered in her kitchen several days after her death when concerned neighbors came to check up on her.

Sometime after the new owners took possession of the house, they began to hear noises and experience "strange sensations." Once, when an interior decorator came to look over the house and suggest some color schemes, an odd thing happened. The decorator was standing in the middle of the living room, holding a large book of wallpaper swatches in his hand. Suddenly, the book was snatched from his hands and literally hurled across the room! He was startled, to say the least.

Then, when the owners selected a shade of soft cream colored paint to be used in painting the upstairs area, and the cans of paint were opened, the paint immediately turned lavender. This happened to several cans and a new batch had to be ordered. When this paint was delivered, the same thing happened again. One room had formerly been painted lavender, and it evidently was the favorite color of the previous owners, who must have been adverse to any change!

Two years after they settled in, our friend's husband passed away. This was in 1986. She now lives alone in the house. Soon after her husband's death, she came home one day to discover that the Seth Thomas clock, which had once belonged to her husband's grandfather, was not in its customary place on the entry hall wall. It was on the floor, over by the staircase. The glass and case were intact, not a scratch to be seen, but the works were now so out of order that the clock had to undergo extensive repair work to get it going again.

Long after her husband passed away, she would detect the fragrance of Aramis, his favorite cologne. It would always be in the area around the staircase. Then, she began to catch fleeting glimpses of a figure passing by a window on the outside of the house as she stood inside. It would be only a glimpse . . . but she knew she had seen someone. A look outside would reveal that no one was there.

Finally, living alone with these uncomfortable manifestations led her to call on a friend who was a Franciscan monk at one of our missions. He came and blessed the house for her. Since the blessing, the house has been more peaceful and calm . . . and so has the owner!

The Ghost That Observed Halloween

On Crofton Street in the King William Historic District, there's an old Victorian two-storied, rambling home that sits on the banks of the river. At one time, before the city "beautified" the river area, there was a lovely garden with trees and flowers that extended down to the banks of the river.

According to a former resident, Mrs. Rosamond Lane, the house was built around 1890 by Mr. T. R. Hertzberg, a prominent citizen who had served as a state senator and had held diplomatic posts at various times in both France and Germany. The Hertzbergs eventually moved to the house next door, and the house was sold to Judge Sidney J. Brooks. His son, Cadet Sidney Brooks, Jr., was the first aviator killed during World War I. He had had a flu shot and was said to have blacked out during a training mission, plummeting to his death. It is for him that Brooks Air Force Base in San Antonio is named. There is a plaque in front of the house proclaiming it to be the "Brooks House," and the name "Brooks" also appears on the cement mounting block by the front curbside. (Mounting blocks were used in horse and buggy days to aid in getting in and out of carriages.)

After his death, Cadet Brooks' casket was placed to lie in state in the front parlor of the house prior to its removal to the old Alamo Methodist Church for the funeral services.

Numerous families have since resided in the house. It was also a boarding house at one time. Mrs. Lane said her father and mother, Mr. and Mrs. Victor Paetznick, bought the house, and this is where Mrs. Lane grew up. She later lived there as an adult with her widowed mother and her own adult children. Mrs. Leta Paetznick left quite a few traces of her personality on the house as well, according to Mrs. Lane. She had a collection of oddly fascinating Madonna paintings which gazed from the walls of the living room and den. Fascinated by the occult, she also left a library of books bearing such titles as *Strange Mysteries of Time and Space*, *Too Many Ghosts*, and *Spooks Deluxe*. Mrs. Paetznick may have been a little psychic, also, as she had premonitions of the violent death of her son,

Victor J., who was killed while serving a tour of duty with the Merchant Marines.

Mrs. Lane had many interesting stories to tell of the old house and the strange happenings that took place there. She doesn't seem to be upset by the events, but rather took them for granted and was quite open about discussing life in the lovely old home, although she now no longer resides there.

Mrs. Lane told us that in April of 1960 she awoke in the early hours of the morning to find a little old lady, dressed in black, sitting on the edge of her bed. Mrs. Lane was pregnant at the time with her youngest son, Jimmy. It had been a difficult pregnancy. She had been very concerned because she had experienced difficulty in delivering her previous children. The old woman told her not to worry, that all would go well, and then went on to tell her the date the new baby would arrive. When she arose, Mrs. Lane noted the date she had been given on the calendar. Little Jimmy arrived exactly on schedule!

Mrs. Lane later found out that when the house had been used as a boarding house, an elderly lady named Clara had occupied the room that was now her bedroom. She is convinced that Clara was the friendly spirit that returned to encourage and assure her that all would go well.

One Halloween, she recalled, when her children were small, she took them out trick-or-treating. They had just returned with their bags of goodies, and set their snack-filled sacks down next to the front door while they went to the den to watch television. Suddenly, the bags started moving, unassisted by human hands. She and her children witnessed the bags as they skidded across the hardwood floors towards the fireplace.

On Halloween night in 1967 "something" pushed a lamp across the floor. Mr. Paetznick also once saw an ax move for a distance of about three feet across a shed behind the house.

She also told us about the time when her brother had passed away in Ohio, and his body was returned to San Antonio for the funeral. All the family had gathered at the house the night before the funeral. Mrs. Lane was sleeping in her upstairs bedroom. Her uncle was in the room across the hall from her, while her parents and brother were sleeping downstairs. All had retired for the night when suddenly, Mrs. Lane heard a very loud "thud" next to her bed. Everyone else heard it also and were awakened by the noise. Then, suddenly, a dog started to howl on the front porch, and simultaneously, other plaintive howls of a dog were heard in her uncle's upstairs bedroom. But when they searched, there were no dogs anywhere to be found!

There were numerous cold spots in the house also, according to Mrs. Lane. She said her son seemed to sense them most often. Once, when he was home on leave from the service, he was going up the stairs to his room when he suddenly yelled. He called to his mother to come and said that someone, or something, had grabbed him by the wrist, and he even had fingernail marks on his wrist to show how hard he had been clutched as he made his way upstairs!

There was another time, when both of her sons were home on a visit. They started playfully "rough-housing" and tussling in an upstairs bedroom much as they had done as little boys. One of her sons' wives was also in the room with them. All of a sudden, all the built-in cabinet doors started opening and closing, banging loudly . . . evidence that the ghost must have wanted them to calm down!

Another visitor seemed to be an "old man" ghost, said Mrs. Lane. He made front door appearances, and once he even playfully tried to get into bed with Mrs. Lanes' mother, Leta Paetznick.

There must have been a pipe-smoker in the house at one time, too, because the aroma of pipe smoke could be detected at times in the house. It seemed to follow a person from room to room. Mr. Paetznick dismissed the smoky smell as leftover odors in the walls, because he said he did not smell the smoke after the house was repapered. In fact, Mrs. Lane said it was probably the change of wallpaper which accounted for fewer appearances in the past few years. "Sometimes when you disturb what is familiar to them, they go away," was her theory.

After living in the house, Mrs. Lane says she believes in ghosts. She received grim predictions in June of 1968 while using a Ouija board. The predictions hinted of an airplane crash that would take place the following month. The prediction came true, and the lives of her ex-husband and two middle sons were claimed.

Now, for a footnote to Mrs. Lane's story. There are new owners in the house now, and a recent conversation with them indicated that something is still there at the old house. The young couple who purchased the property are doing quite a bit of restoring and renovating. They were a little reluctant to talk about it, lest the skeptical among our readers laugh at them. They did, however, share a couple of events that took place soon after they settled in.

For one thing, a calendar on the wall literally flew off the wall one day. Then, there was a strange occurrence that took place in the kitchen.

There was a shortage of built-in cabinets in the kitchen, so they decided to place hooks under the existing cabinets from which to hang pots and pans and various cooking utensils, including a colander. After one evening of hard work, the couple had a little disagreement about something and the husband left the kitchen and stomped upstairs to bed. Still a little steamed up, his wife elected to remain in the kitchen to "cool off." She said she turned on the small television set in the kitchen and settled down at the kitchen table to watch a late night show on TV. Suddenly, the colander, which was hanging on one of the newly placed hooks, was hurled across the room and landed right at her feet. She said if it had just fallen, it would have landed on the counter . . . but no . . . it literally flew across the room! She said it was as if the resident spirit was saying . . . "oh cool off . . . stop being stupid . . . and go on up to bed!" She said she just sat and took a deep breath, then replaced the colander on its hook beneath the cabinet, turned out the light, and went upstairs to bed. She said she believes the spirit is very benevolent, friendly, and most of all, pretty sensible!

The Haunted Sea Captain's House

Our interest was first aroused a number of years ago, when a special article, entitled, "A Haunting We Will Go" appeared in the Sunday Magazine section of the *San Antonio Express-News*. On Sunday, October 28, 1984, Niki Frances McDaniel, a regular *News* writer, reported how she had gone so far as to spend the night in a reputed-to-be-haunted house.

When we started looking for the house she described in the article . . . some six years ago . . . we simply could not locate it. Her descriptions of the location indicated it was out by the Salado Creek near the Austin Highway on what used to be part of the old Tobin estate. Of course, we were looking for the house as it was pictured and described in the McDaniel article. It was then noted as an old stone house sitting off the road in a stand of trees, in the midst of natural brush and cow pastures. What a difference just a few years can make!

When we finally located the house, we found it totally encircled by an exclusive apartment complex, almost hidden from view unless one knew just where to look. On private

property, it is not a place that can today be visited by the casual drop-in visitor (or ghost-hunter!) as it was at the time the *News* article was printed.

We were, however, graciously received by the apartment complex management when we explained we were doing some research on San Antonio's haunted houses, and the young ladies in the office even went so far as to unlock the latticed doorway into the half basement beneath the structure so we could walk around and view that area in the filtered light that comes in from the open windows.

It is evident that the house has been greatly altered from its initial appearance, but at least the apartment complex owners valued it enough to preserve it, even though not in the original state. The old house was almost square, in the early "dog trot" style, with a central hallway. There was a door to the outside on either end of the hallway, and the house was divided into two large rooms. The walls dividing the dog trot from the rooms have been removed and today the house is just one large room. Funny, we didn't notice a fireplace, but perhaps there was one, or even two, one in each room, that may have been sealed up. After all, how could a homesteader have survived without one? The walls in the interior have been cleaned of any paint or stucco that might once have covered them, and are just the exposed natural limestone. Faint lines can be seen where the walls of the two rooms were removed.

Also, there must have been an attic, or loft, but that too has been removed so that one may look clear up to the roof. The cross beams still bear nail marks from the former attic floor. The house today faces on a peaceful and attractive little patio filled with fragrant plantings, and we surmised it is now used for a meeting place or party house for the apartment complex dwellers.

So peaceful . . . so pretty . . . but the story, heard in various versions, and seen in print in several articles (another *Express News* article printed October 29, 1989 again made mention of the house) certainly causes the prickles to come up on one's skin. And we did feel a certain amount of discomfort in the basement, especially . . . nothing, mind you, we could actually put a finger on . . . we just didn't like being there . . . .

You see, the old house was built on land that was once considered to be sacred by the Indians, near the Salado Creek that was long a tribal gathering place. Several battles later on took place along the creek banks. The house stood right on the old Camino Real . . . the "Royal Road" that led out of San Antonio to the Spanish settlements in East Texas.

Ancient lands . . . old turmoils . . . legends embedded in time . . . and an old house that was a part of it all.

We will quote parts of the story as so well told in the article by McDaniel:

"About a century ago, a sea captain from up East, Boston or somewhere, decided to get out of seafaring and buy himself a ranch in Texas. So, he collected his savings, sold his ship, and came West. He found a site he liked on Salado Creek, about a half days' ride from the cowtown that was San Antonio then, on the old Camino Real.

"There, he bought some land and built a house out of cut limestone, nothing fancy, but an airy, well-lighted, solid structure, situated to make the most of the southerly breezes blowing up toward the hills. The sea captain built his house with sort of a half basement, situated only partly underground. The basement floor was plain dirt, but there were windows at eye level all the way around for plentiful light and air.

"A stairway led up to the second level, really the main floor, which was divided into two large, symmetrical rooms connected by a dog run. Each of these main-floor rooms had high ceilings and giant windows on three walls, affording a pleasant view from half a story above the ground. Over the main level was an attic running all the way across the top of the house, with windows at each end. It didn't have a lot of head space, but it would do nicely for children's quarters.

"Once the sea captain's house was built and his ranch was operating he realized something was missing. So, he hightailed it back to Boston and married a beautiful young Boston belle. She was some years younger than he, but enthralled, no doubt, with his adventurous past and his present dash and daring. After the ceremony, they packed up all her trunks and finery and headed for San Antonio, their new home. But once they got there, the honeymoon didn't last for long . . . ." In the sea captain's day, Salado Creek was out in the sticks in a serious way. Neighbors were miles distant. One could not merely gallop off to San Antonio to relieve the loneliness and drudgery of frontier life . . . there was too much work to be done. And even if there hadn't been, San Antonio hardly could offer the kind of stimulation a Boston belle of culture and refinement would be seeking.

"So, the sea captain's wife was unhappy. She was lonely and bored and miserable. She began to suggest they go East again. The captain didn't take her seriously at first. His life savings were tied up in that ranch and that house, and it was beginning to look as though he really might make a go of things. She would learn to love the place, in time . . . .

"Time went by, and the captain and his wife quarreled. Then she cried and begged him to take her away. But he was resolute, he would not leave. She grew more and more miserable, and she was even lonelier now . . . they barely got along at all. He was furious and hurt. This was his dream. How could she reject it?

"Finally, she told him she was leaving without him. He wouldn't hear of it. In rage and frustration, he lashed out and knocked her down. She hit her head on the foot-thick limestone rock wall of the house he had built so lovingly. And she never woke up.

"He buried her in the basement and covered the dirt floor with a limestone slab . . . and it's said you can hear the sea captain's wife still weeping out behind the house where the cow shed used to be. It's said the house is full of strange lights on dark nights when the moon is new. It's said that later occupants of the house never lived there very long. They were disturbed by the sound of the sea captain dragging his dead wife down to the basement, her head going thump, thump, thump, on the stairs."

Well, that's the story. The apartment manager and her assistant had not heard it before. They knew the house was very old, of course, but the tale of its being haunted had never reached them.

Come to think of it . . . they said . . . it WAS very difficult to lease the apartment closest to the old house. They said the price had even been lowered, but no one would stay there for some reason. And, just as we were leaving, the young lady who had shown us around said, "You know, it is strange, but some nights when I'm here alone in the office, working late, the lights will go on and off for no apparent reason at all, and I always feel a little bit uneasy . . . ."

The House of Hope

Motorists driving in the fast lane down Perrin-Beitel Road, north of Loop 410 in San Antonio, drive right past one of the community's oldest and most interesting landmarks, and probably do not even notice it. For, sitting just behind the Swan's Landing Shopping Center is a historic property, looking very much as it must have when it was built in 1871.

Intrigued by its appearance, and wanting to know more about the place, we approached the current owner, Mr. Seymour J. Dreyfus. He was kind enough to share a copy of a thesis written by Tim Swan, son of a former owner, which was entitled, "Hope Farm, A Century of Change." From it we gained much interesting data, including the fact that once upon a time the Hope Farm house was haunted!

The builder-designer of the house, which was centered in 504 acres of fine farmland, was Alphonse Perrin. He was the son of French parents who had immigrated to New York by way of Switzerland. In his early days as a young man he went to sea on a freighter (1861) and remained in this line of work for about four years. His family said he didn't even know there had been a Civil War until he returned! In 1865 he went to visit some friends in Wisconsin and there he met a lovely young woman, Mina Carr, whom he later married.

During the years he spent as a seaman, Alphonse had contracted the deadly disease tuberculosis. For a time he went to Florida, and then later he came to Texas, to try and regain his strength and health. Texas seemed to be the answer, for in a couple of years he had become well and strong. He then traveled by horseback to St. Louis, and from there took a train to Milwaukee to claim his lovely fiancee. The couple were married in Chicago and then came to Texas via a trip down the Mississippi River. When they first arrived, they settled in the little community of Leon Springs. However, Alphonse was anxious to find a good-sized tract of land, which he could farm and where he could rear a family. He searched for quite some time before locating what he wanted. A Mr. Judson contacted him from Massachusetts. He was the absentee owner of the land northeast of San Antonio and since he did not live in the area, he was willing to sell it. Alphonse examined the property, some 35 miles from where he and Mina were living, and decided it would make excellent farmland. It was located near the Salado Creek, whose limestone banks would yield the stone of which the house was to be built. After purchasing the property, Alphonse set to work designing the house himself. French stonemasons were brought from New York to cut and prepare the stones which would form the sturdy, strong walls of his new home. Doors and windows were sent all the way from New York, coming first to Galveston by boat, and then overland to San Antonio by wagon.

Mina and Alphonse moved into their new home in 1871. There they lived and prospered and raised six children. Their first child, Alphonse Thomas, was born September 14, 1871. The infant only lived fourteen days.

The stone house was added onto several times as the family grew. When describing the house to a friend in a letter, Mina wrote, "It will be a delightful home when finished. Please God we may live and die here."

The farm on which the house was situated was named Hope Farm and the family enjoyed a number of years of happiness and prosperity while living there. Mina died in 1912, while Alphonse survived her and lived until October 18, 1922, thus fulfilling Mina's wish they live and die in the house. He was buried beside his wife and the first infant son who had died, in a little family cemetery which is about 300 yards to the northeast of the house (it is located on Perrin Beitel Road).

After Alphonse died, the family attorney and husband of one of the Perrin daughters, Martha, began dividing up the land on Hope Farm. This lawyer was named M. C. Judson. Because of the settlement among the heirs, the farm was subdivided and sold for the first time. A portion of the acreage was purchased by a Mr. Serna, who donated 100 acres for the establishment of a school district. The school was called North East School and was the first school in what is today the Northeast School District. The first school was replaced in 1950 by a new building, which was called the Serna Elementary School.

First industry, then subdivisions and various small businesses took up some of the land as the city moved northward, until there wasn't much left of old Hope Farm. In 1964 Mrs. Margaret Swan found the old house, now showing signs of neglect and wear. There were eight acres surrounding the place. The walls of the house were still sturdy, and the floor plan airy and inviting. It just needed lots of love and fixing up, which the Swans were willing to do. There was land, too, for Mrs. Swan to build a swimming pool for training her famous synchronized swimming team, the San Antonio Cygnets. The Swans restored the house and were able to buy much of the old furniture which had belonged to the Perrin family. They did, however, have to rearrange and remodel some of the rooms to better suit their needs. For the work they did on the house they were honored with it being designated a Texas historical landmark in 1969.

During the first couple of years the Swans resided in the house, as they were slowly restoring and remodeling, they were bothered by a lot of unexplainable happenings. Doors would open and close, and they would hear footsteps echoing on the old hardwood floors. Windows would rattle, and boxes would be opened. Beds, and sometimes their occupants, would be disturbed. The old Perrin home seemed to have a ghost! These disturbances went on for some time, more than likely because the spirit did not want the house to be remodeled. At last things settled down, and there have been no reports of ghostly visits in recent years. If the ghost was Mina, she must have realized the "delightful home" she described had been lovingly and carefully restored, and so she was pleased and went on to her eternal rest.

The Swans have since sold the house. It is currently occupied, but the property, which is owned by Mr. Seymour Dreyfus, is for sale. It still looks sturdy. Its long front porch is cool and inviting, and there is a charming bay window on the side of the house that would be the perfect spot for a morning cup of coffee or an afternoon spot of tea. Years-old trees provide a canopy of shade to the front of the house. The old Hope Farm house is just waiting for someone to come along and love it again!

Leon Valley's Storied Stagecoach Stop

Along a busy stretch of Bandera Road, in the northwest community of Leon Valley, there's an old stone house. Situated just south of where Poss Road crosses Bandera, the place sits, forlorn and deserted, on what must be several acres of heavily wooded land. The yard is overgrown with weeds, and on the lower floor the windows are all boarded up. The door stands ajar, allowing a view right through the house. There's a gate leading into the driveway, but it too stands ajar.

A rusted old bedstead leans against the front porch wall. The upper porch was once screened in, but now great torn, rusty pieces of screening hang suspended from the eaves and sides in tumbled disarray. The upstairs windows and doors are dark, like great, closed eyes afraid to glimpse the sunlight. Only the sturdy walls of limestone and the tall chimney show the strength that this house once possessed, for it has truly suffered from vandalism, neglect, and the ravages that natural elements have wreaked upon it.

This is a house with a story . . . or several stories. All are worth the telling. It is a house that deserves to be restored, to come alive again to offer shelter beneath its roof and warmth beside its empty hearth.

It is called the Old Onion House by some, but the Onion family only owned it after 1930. It was built of native limestone in 1848, and was first owned by a Mr. Joseph Huebner and his family. Later, it was occupied by the family of Andres and Felipa Salazar, early Leon Valley settlers, who rented it about 1911. The house was then owned by a Judge Taliaferro, from whom Judge John F. Onion and his wife, Harriet, purchased it in 1930. Mrs. Onion had been wanting to move to the country for sometime, as she considered it a better place to bring up her twin boys, Jim and John. They were about five years old at the time the property was purchased, and in Mrs. Onion's words, "very active."

We decided to do some investigating as we had heard strange rumors of unexplained happenings taking place in the old house. An article in the *San Antonio Express News* on October 31, 1984 led us to contact Mr. Ken Alley, former mayor of Leon Valley and a noted historian. Mr. Alley possesses a tape recording of a talk that the late Mrs. Harriet Onion made to the Leon Valley Historical Society, which he kindly played for us. It was from the information derived from the tape, our talk with Mr. and Mrs. Alley, and the *Express News* article that we have gleaned most of our information.

At the time the Onions purchased the property, it included thirteen acres of land. The house was then about eighty years old. When they moved in, there were no windows on the north side. This helped to keep out the cold in the winter and made fewer windows to defend against Indian attacks. The Onions found several musket balls shot into the walls and lodged between the stones, indicating a certain amount of "activity" there in the early days.

At first the Onions just "camped" there, spending some time in the summers and on weekends, but as they slowly got the place fixed up, they spent more and more time there, finally making it their permanent residence.

So, it was there, in Leon Valley, that the twin boys grew up and attended school. The boys lived there until the 1950s. Mrs. Onion lived on in the house after Judge Onion died in 1955.

She left shortly before her death in March 1983, which was just after her ninetieth birthday.

When Mrs. Onion told her friends they were buying the old house on Bandera Road, many wondered why and asked her if she was sure she wanted to buy a house reputed to be haunted.

It seems there were stories abroad that when wagons crossed the Huebner Creek, the drivers would have to whip the horses to get them to pass by the place quickly because of the strange noises coming from the house.

Mrs. Onion attributed the ghostly noises to a family of screech owls that made their home in the attic, under the eaves. She said at the beginning her worst problems were with the rattlesnakes that inhabited the surrounding property. She said she killed "65 or 70" of the critters, and the most recent one she said had been a six-foot, eight pounder with ten rattles on his "warning device" whom she had dispatched with a snub-nosed .38 revolver. She laughingly said she'd shot it in the back, but that it was an "accident."

Although they had been told the house was haunted at the time of purchase, they made light of the stories, until they began to hear so many unusual noises and experience so many strange occurrences that could not be traced to the screech owls, that they knew something, or someone, was truly there in the house with them.

"We heard some of the weirdest noises you ever heard," Mrs. Onion said on the tape. "Some of the things are just too weird to tell." There was the time the family heard a tremendous crash from the dining room. "One night it sounded like the china cabinet had turned over," she said. "I got my little pistol (a snub-nosed .38, probably her snake killer weapon) and went downstairs to find nobody there. Everything was in perfect order, at least in as much order as I ever kept anything."

Her son Jim, the twin of Judge John Onion, recalled the incident, too. "We had a guest staying upstairs and we heard this glass shattering. It had to be the china closet because it sounded like a lot of glass breaking. Our guest sat straight up in her bed and said, What's that? What's that? My mom got her gun and they went downstairs and they found the china cabinet right there, upright." They never did discover the source of the noise and commotion.

Some nights the family would hear squeaks on the stairs. "Sometimes they would go to the boys' room; sometimes they would come towards our room and then just go down the hall." Mrs. Onion said they always tried to make light of the sounds, because the hired help would not have stayed if they had appeared afraid, and "the boys would have grown up idiots if they had thought about ghosts all the time."

On the recording, Mrs. Onion also told about being alone in the living room one time and hearing a loud chord being played on the piano, which was in the room with her. Then, she said once, when she and her husband were alone in the house at night, the boys having grown up and left home, they heard the distinct sounds of little children running and playing upstairs. She said the sounds were very real. Of course, when they went upstairs to investigate, there was no one there.

In the early days, soon after the house was constructed, the stagecoach route from San Antonio passed through Leon Valley enroute to Helotes, Bandera, and points west. The Huebner house was said to be the first stop out of San Antonio on this stage route. Here horses were changed in the old barn out back. A regular mail route existed as early as 1867, also. In those days, most of the ranches in the area, which was then considered to be part of Helotes, were in constant danger from Indian attacks. The ranchers all went heavily armed as a consequence.

Leon Valley was considered a dangerous area for wagons and stagecoaches because the hills were steep, there were two creeks to cross, and the ground was often muddy. If a wagon bogged down in the mud and got stuck, the occupants were in danger of attacks from either Indians or robbers. According to early newspaper accounts many holdups were alleged to have been staged by robbers who made their hideaway in the old Robert's Cave, fourteen miles northwest of San Antonio, on what is now Babcock Road. On one occasion, ten unidentified bandits jumped a stagecoach headed for Helotes, killed everyone aboard, and made off with $60,000 in cash.

Mrs. Onion said that Judge Taliaferro had told her of a legend that there was some gold buried on the place. (This might have been the ill-gotten booty from the stage robbery.) At any rate, she said one time some men came to the house and asked permission to dig on the land out behind the house.

Chapter 3

They were granted permission and they dug a very large hole as young Jim and John watched them work. The men told the boys they were very hot and thirsty, and would they please get them some water to drink. The boys went to the house for water, and when they returned, the diggers had all their shirts and jackets off, "bunched up like they were hiding something in them," and, then announced they had finished digging and headed off. Whether they had found something and made a hasty retreat, or just given up, no one knows.

Now, we have established there was a ghost . . . or maybe more than one . . . but who was it? The Onions and most other people familiar with the history of the house are convinced it was the ghost of "Old Man Huebner," the occupant of the house way back when it was a stagecoach stop. Although some stories vary, all seem to be in agreement that Joseph Huebner "imbibed." The story goes that a mule train once stopped over at the Huebner place. They needed Mr. Huebner, who was a good blacksmith and also somewhat of a self-taught veterinarian in the days when animal doctors were almost unheard of, to tend to shoeing some of the mules and doctoring one which was sick. Nobody knows for sure the year this all happened. But the story is that Mr. Huebner worked on the mule awhile, and imbibed awhile. Seems the mule train was carrying a big load of whiskey.

The tale that has been passed on is that he got so drunk he mistook a jug of kerosene ("coal oil" they called it back then) for a jug of whiskey. He was a big man, but he managed to get back into the house and onto his mattress, where he is said to have "expired" soon thereafter. Only thing is they weren't sure if he was dead, or just "dead drunk." But the community voted him dead, and he was hastily dispatched to a grave they dug at the rear of the property on the north banks of Huebner Creek. There is still a broken grave marker there somewhere among the tangle of weeds and underbrush. (There is also the grave of an infant baby girl in the same area.)

If the old rancher wasn't actually dead when he was put six feet under might just explain the hauntings. Strangely enough, the ghostly noises abruptly stopped in 1955, the year that Mrs. Onion's husband, Judge John F. Onion, passed away. Even though he was a heavy drinker, maybe old Joseph Huebner was somewhat of a gentleman in his own way. Maybe he just decided it wasn't quite fair to keep on scaring a lone

144

lady who had, after all, tended his old house and property with loving care all those years of her occupancy. Her husband was gone, and there was no one left to bolster her courage when those frightening noises began. Old Joseph must have decided to quietly settle down for good, in that spot down on the banks of the creek, so Mrs. Onion could live out her final days in the house in peace and quiet.

Chapter 3

The House That Sam Built

In the exclusive Terrill Hills residential area, there's a house on a shady street that has a "live-in" resident whom the owner has named "Sam." Actually, Sam was probably the builder of the house. He had built it to be his dream home, but his girlfriend backed out of the engagement, refusing to marry him, and he was left devastated, with a new home and a shattered dream. This proved to be too much for him, and so he went away soon afterwards and committed suicide. But he has never been able to give up that dream entirely, and so he keeps coming back. Therein lies a story.

We first learned about the house from a former tenant, who has since passed away. He had resided there for about two years, while the owner was away in another city on business. This young man, whom we will call "Bill," told us several interesting stories concerning the house. His little dog would get very agitated at night . . . and would bark and run around the house. His hair would stand up along his back and neck, as if he were undergoing great fright. Bill would get up and look around the house but would find no one there.

An art collector, he had a wall of paintings displayed on the dining room wall, many highlighted with portrait lights. Several times, he said, he would come into the dining room upon arising and find a chair pulled back from the dining table, facing the wall of pictures, as if someone had been sitting there admiring the art work. The lights would also be turned on over the paintings, although he was quite positive he had turned them all off before retiring.

Bill said he had a collection of treasured glass and crystal animals he displayed on his coffee table. Often he would find them rearranged, and even placed on other tables about the room. Sam is undoubtedly an art lover!

Several times Bill would be awakened at night by the rustling of shrubbery outside his bedroom window. (He occupied a front bedroom.) He would check and find nothing there, but the rustling continued, night after night, disturbing his rest. Finally, in exasperation, one night he said in a loud voice ". . . whoever you are, if you want to live here, that's fine . . .

maybe it was your house, but either be quiet or get the ___ out of here because I simply have to get some sleep." He said whoever, or whatever, it was, calmed down, and he didn't hear anything for a couple of months. He also found that the front bedroom was always cold . . . even on warm nights. Finally, he decided to change sleeping quarters, moving to a back bedroom where he was never disturbed.

Bill had a friend who was moving to San Antonio. While he was relocating and apartment hunting he decided to spend some time with Bill as a houseguest. Well, that was the plan. But after two nights, he told Bill he didn't know what it was about that house, but he couldn't sleep, and there was "something wrong" there that surely did disturb him. He said he just couldn't stay in that room because he heard footsteps, but no one was there, and he was very disturbed. End of visit.

When we talked to the owner, who now lives in the house with just his dog, he told us that Sam is definitely still around. He said on numerous occasions he has heard footsteps in the hall outside the front bedroom where he sleeps. The dog has barked and growled and dashed out into the hallway. He said one night recently he saw what he described as a "green mist, like a patch of fog" outside the bedroom door. Recently, when he had to be away on business, he had a young man come to stay in the house as a house sitter. This young man also saw the same "green fog" in the hallway. The owner still remains there. He says after all it is his house, and he just has to accept Sam, who just hangs around, keeping an eye on things. Maybe he is still seeking the happiness he had hoped to have there, and never realized.

There Was Something About
That House . . . .

When Roy Williams and I were married in 1984, we decided the best thing to do would be to sell both of our houses, pool our resources, and buy "our" house.

We began a search for just the right, perfect house, where we could spend all the rest of our days, and that search took a couple of years. We would find a house we liked, but we wouldn't like the yard, or the neighborhood, or we felt it was over our budget . . . seemed like we just couldn't find what we wanted.

At last, I viewed a house with a realtor that I felt would meet our needs, but unfortunately the asking price was just a bit too steep at the time. The house was large . . . a one-story stucco house on a tree shaded street in the prestigious Terrill Hills area. The neighborhood was settled . . . most of the houses must be twenty or thirty years old in that section. But this was a new house.

I noticed, however, the yard was in, there were tall trees, and evidence of "old" landscaping. It was definitely not a "new" yard.

I told the realtor I would think it over and then let the matter drop. Several months later, she called to tell me it had been reduced in price and asked would I now be interested. I went back for another look and then took my husband and a good friend along to look at it.

It had so many of the qualities we really wanted, including a very spacious "great room" for entertaining. But there was one thing I couldn't quite put my finger on . . . it had a marble entryway and a fireplace that didn't look new, like the rest of the house. I was assured, however, it was a new structure. We finally settled on a price and the earnest money was paid. The only thing . . . I kept getting a funny feeling about that house. I would go by to look at the windows, figuring how many would require drapes, and where I could place my furniture, and each time I went I would get sort of an uneasy feeling about the house.

Finally, the day came when we were to settle the deal with the bank. The night before, I tossed and turned. I honestly felt sick. I did . . . and I didn't . . . want to move into that house. The morning I was to give our check to the realtor I went back over one more time, with my husband, to look around. The night before a big crack must have occurred in the wall of the breakfast room, and in the doorway to the great room, and there was a good bit of plaster all over the floor. I became really distressed over buying a house that was evidently settling, and worried about what else might go wrong.

This time the realtor told me that she had heard that the house was built on the site of a former house that had burned down. This would explain the older-looking marble entry and the fireplace. But this worried me because I knew old foundations and old plumbing might still be part of the house. It wasn't like me to get so upset . . . here I was, on the brink of buying our "dream home" and I discovered I really didn't want it after all. Also, I had been having a strange feeling whenever I would walk into one of the front bedrooms.

Even though it was August, I always felt cold in that room. And I had had a couple of really spooky nightmares, relating to the house. I had just attributed these to "paying-a-lot-of-money-for-a-new-house jitters."

The end result was that right on the day of the final settlement, we canceled out on the deal, losing our earnest money, of course. Later on, my husband talked to a friend on the Terrill Hills police force, telling him we had almost bought a house in that area. When he asked, "Where?" and my husband told him, he said, "Oh, I remember that place. That's where the lady burned up alive in her house . . . such a tragedy." Evidently, the former owner had been smoking in bed and dropped off to sleep . . . at least that was what was believed to have happened. Anyway, the house and the owner were both destroyed in the fire, and the new house was constructed on the old foundation, utilizing the still standing fireplace and lovely old entryway. I always wondered if the place where she had died was in the location of the front bedroom where I experienced the cold chills!

The house is now occupied, and I hope the new owners have never experienced any uneasiness. It is a lovely house, but it just wasn't meant to belong to us.

The Midget Mansion

We first heard about the house that was known as Midget Mansion from our friend Reba Marshall. She had vivid memories of the old house which was located in the area where she had lived as a youngster. She told us it was on Donore, off Frederickburg Road. She said she had heard the house, which was a large building of native limestone, had been built by a former naval officer. She told us in those days it was considered to be out in the country, and Donore Street was cut through later on. The house burned some years ago, leaving only the walls standing. A large swimming pool was in the back of the house.

Reba said she believed the house was built in the 1920s, or perhaps a little earlier. The story she told us is very strange, but one she had heard and believed since she was a little girl. It seems the house came into the hands of a successful businessman, who happened to be a midget. Reba says he may have been in the insurance business. He had a wife, also very small, but their two children were normal size. They lived quite happily, until the husband suddenly went berserk and went on a mad rampage. The story went that he slit the throats of his family and stuffed them all in a closet. Later on he took them out, cleaned them up, dressed them in clean clothes, and replaced them in the closet. Then, we are told, he is supposed to have shot himself.

There were bloody handprints all over the inside of the closet when police found the bodies, indicating they must have been still alive when first placed there. Over the years, subsequent occupants reported hearing scratchings on the walls and moans in the house.

The house finally became vacant and it is said that a satanic cult held some of their meetings there. Carcasses of dead cats and dogs, apparently slaughtered in some sort of ritual killings, were found in the empty swimming pool, and satanic symbols and writings were everywhere.

Finally, the pool was filled in and the last remaining walls were pulled down. All that can be seen from Donore Street today is a closed wire mesh fence with a padlock on the gate.

The gate spans a long driveway, the sides of which are over-grown with weeds and overhanging trees, and a hedge of dense bamboo. There are still several large mansions in the general neighborhood. Perhaps one day another home will occupy the site of what is still referred to as the "Midget Mansion" . . . the grounds are up for sale!

The House That Was
Once a Funeral Parlor

A friend of ours, Kathy Hendrix, told us of an old house she knew about in Boerne. The house stood somewhere near the river. She said an elderly lady who lived there had reported several strange occurrences. One of the strangest was when she had another lady in to tea one afternoon. As they sat in the front parlor, her visitor looked up and saw a man pass through the hallway in her line of vision. She told her hostess, "Oh, I didn't know you had another visitor." Her hostess assured her that she did not; they were quite alone in the house.

Later on, the man was seen in the hallway, which was just outside the bathroom, on several occasions. The lady who lived there found out the house had at one time served as a funeral parlor. Perhaps the gentlemen visitor was the "friendly undertaker" just come back to check up on things. At any rate, his unscheduled visits were sufficiently upsetting that the occupant had a priest come in on three different occasions to read exorcism prayers, and there have been no more reports of the house being haunted.

The Old Mission Ranch House

The October 31, 1984 edition of the *San Antonio Express News* reported that the old Spanish ranch house near the Mission Concepcion is haunted. This is what the article stated:

"Strange noises still persist at another ranch house, just south of downtown San Antonio. The owner still lives there, has no intention of moving, and believes about ghosts: 'They don't hurt you . . . they just scare you.' Bob, who didn't want his full name printed, has restored the old Mission Concepcion ranch house to its 18th century grandeur. Filled with Spanish and Mexican accoutrements, Bob's home gives new meaning to the term, 'restoration.' Some three hundred soldiers died in that area during an 18th century battle near the mission. A Dr. Navarro, who lived there around the turn of the century, is said to have murdered Juana, who was either his live-in maid or his lover. Nobody knows for sure. In any case, Bob, who was repeating a rosary . . . 'I only know it in Spanish . . . I never learned it in English' . . . saw a plume of smoke waft in from a back room. Forming a column in front of him, it didn't take on masculine or feminine features, he said, but simply stood and watched him. He moved towards the apparition and it disappeared. Going back to his rosary, the column of smoke reappeared."

When Peggy Met the Priest

We have a friend named Peggy, who is a very rational and intelligent lady. She told us a story that, because she told it, we believe. She resided in a prestigious apartment complex on the north side several years ago with her then twelve-year-old daughter. One night the youngster was away spending the night with friends and Peggy had just settled into bed in her upstairs bedroom. She heard footsteps coming up the steps. She sat up in bed, from where she could see the stairway from her bedroom door. She saw the upper part of a man, "dressed in the dark brown robes of a priest" . . . with a hood over his head and a "rope tied around his waist" as the figure came slowly up the stairs. The apparition floated past her bedroom door and seemed to go into her daughter's room next door. Knowing, yet not knowing, what she had seen, Peggy said she was so terrified she couldn't get up . . . she just pulled the covers over her head and lay there for what seemed like hours, too frightened to get up and look around. When she finally did get up, there was nothing there in the apartment.

She didn't mention this to her daughter for fear of frightening the child. But several days later, her child asked her, "Mama, have you ever seen a ghost?" Peggy told her she thought she had, but did not offer any other information. She was astounded when her daughter went on to tell her that she had been in the bathroom brushing her teeth and, as she looked up at the mirror, saw a man "dressed like a priest, with a hood up over his head" looking at her. When she turned around, of course, there was no one there. The mother-daughter pair never saw the figure again, but then they didn't remain in the apartment much longer, either!

Peggy said she heard later that the apartments were built over the site of an old country cemetery, but she could never find out for sure if this was true.

The House in Monte Vista

Rosamond Lane, who used to live in the old Brooks House, also told us she recalled having visited another house which was haunted. This one is located in the old historic Monte Vista District, next to a large church. She was told by the owners the story of how, when painters were redoing the house at their orders, a lady suddenly appeared in the room where a painter was working. She told him she did not like the color he was painting the room. He told her he was very sorry, but he was working under the instructions of the new owners, and this was the color they had selected. The lady then started walking towards him. When she got to the big dining table which stood in the middle of the room, she didn't go around it; she walked right through it, towards him! The painter is reported to have thrown down his paint brush and left in one big hurry. He did not return to finish the job.

Grandpa Was There

Our friend Milton Schelper, who lives on Dinn Avenue on the northeast side, had several interesting stories to share with us. In 1990 his wife's father passed away. "Grandpa" and his wife lived on Josephine Avenue. His wife was an invalid, confined to a wheelchair. She couldn't walk at all and had to be helped into her chair. So when her husband passed away at home, she could not get out of her chair and get to a phone to call for help. The poor old lady sat in her wheelchair, with her dead husband in the house, for a day and a night, just hoping that someone would come. Milton's wife, Mary, was concerned when no one answered the telephone at her parents' house and went over to the house to check up on them. That is when she discovered her father was dead and her mother was still just "sitting and waiting . . . ."

Mary took her mother home with her, and from the time she arrived in the house, Milton says strange unexplained things started to happen. The first night she was there, and every night thereafter for about three weeks, loud noises came from the backyard area. Milton finally realized it was someone, or something, hitting the metal barbecue smoker. He noticed the metal brush he kept with it kept disappearing and reappearing, and he decided that was what was being hit against the smoker. When he would go outside the noise would stop. As soon as he got back into the house it would start up again. His dog was afraid to go out in the yard. Wood that was piled in the yard would be dropped on the patio and they could hear it hitting, but never could find out who, or what, was causing it to be dropped. For weeks the light in Milton's workshed out back would go on and off. He said he knew he always turned the lights out but they would just go on and off at will.

Then, the manifestations moved into the house. Milton first felt a very cold breeze or draft in the hall of the house even though there was no wind blowing outside and the temperature was around eighty degrees. He said it wasn't cool . . . it was downright cold, and it would come on all of a sudden.

Milton said he plugged in an electric drill to do some work in the house and the drill caught fire. He unplugged it and checked the wall plug, then plugged in another drill, and it wouldn't work either. The next day he went in to work on the wall plug since he still felt it might be faulty. This time when he plugged in the drills, and also a radio, everything worked fine.

About two weeks after the strange things started occurring, when Milton arrived home from work he saw a man dressed in a blue shirt and gray pants standing on the porch. As he walked towards the figure, it literally "burst into a hundred tiny pieces" and disappeared. Convinced something was either terribly wrong or he was going out of his mind, Milton finally talked to a medium. He thought maybe he could get in touch with whatever it was and ask it to leave. He even asked about buying a Ouija board. The medium told him they were something people should not get involved with, and that often poltergeists and unfriendly spirits get into them, and he had best forget that idea.

About three weeks after the death of Mary Schelper's father, her mother had to be moved to a nursing home. Evidently, seeing she was being well cared for, "Grandpa" decided to rest in peace and there have been no strange noises or other unusual events since then. Mary's mother soon passed away also, and Milton and Mary just hope they are now happy because they are together.

Milton told us another story, since we were discussing ghosts. He said when he was a youngster, his grandmother was very ill . . . in fact, she was dying. The family sent for her son, who was in the Navy, to come home. He had notified them he would be arriving by train. They had told the sick old lady that her son was on the train and would be home soon to see her. Just then, Milton said, they all heard a shrill train whistle . . . it sounded as if the train was right outside the house. At that very moment, Milton's grandmother died. It was several hours later when her son arrived, by train, too late to see his mother still alive. The house was "miles from the nearest railroad track, and we had never, ever, heard a train whistle at that location . . . never before, or since." Milton also told us about some friends of his in Bulverde who built a home over an area that was said to have been an old Indian burial ground. Soon after they moved in, the wife went outside to hang some laundry out to dry and discovered when she got back to the house she was locked out. She had to get in through a window. This continued until she finally kept a key in her pocket whenever she would go out the door. Both the front and back doors would lock themselves. She said the pictures in the house were always crooked no matter how often they were straightened.

And this is really strange . . . their little girl kept telling them "I see an Indian outside." They never saw this, but the child continues to still see "the Indian" periodically!

Owls That Screeched and Floors That Creaked

Allen Turner, a former staff writer for the *San Antonio Light*, wrote an interesting account of a San Antonio haunting several years ago that was entitled, "Researchers to Follow Ghostly Trail in San Antonio." In his article, Turner referred to the couple involved as "Mr. and Mrs. B" to protect their privacy. Their former residence, from which they fled after several years, was haunted with various spirits, including what they believed was a poltergeist.

The story goes that an elderly woman, the wife of the original owner, was forced out of her home by her family. The first time that "Mrs. B" visited the place, attracted by a For Sale sign in the yard, she was met at the front door by the woman who lived there. The woman was armed with a shotgun and accompanied by a ferocious-looking German shepherd. Mrs. B was told to leave the premises because the house was NOT for sale. Mrs. B persevered, however, and contacted the realtors. Consequently, a deal was struck, the old lady was forced to move out, and the "B's" moved in. The old lady died just about a month after the house was purchased.

From the day they moved in, strange things began to happen. Unknowingly, the "B's" selected the room in which the first owner had died to be their master bedroom. That first night an owl screeched loudly, first inside, then outside, of the room. The sounds grew louder and louder, and although they searched, they could not find the source of the noises. They moved to another bedroom, but still they were disturbed. First, they would hear the floor creaking as footsteps would be heard in the bedroom, outside in the hallway, and on the stairs. Windows would open and shut. The light switches would flip on and off although no one was standing near them. And, most frightening of all, they began to see strange faces peering at them from upstairs windows when they would leave the locked house!

Once, when Mrs. B was in her yard, she was startled to see a middle-aged man wearing overalls blocking her path. As she approached him, he disappeared. Consequently, she saw him on several more occasions.

The "B's" believe the strange happenings were all related to the lady who was ousted from her home by her family. Perhaps the man they saw had been her husband or another relative. After she died, they are certain her spirit returned to try and frighten them away because they had taken over her beloved home. She was trying to make her presence known so she could drive them out. She was apparently successful, because they did sell out and moved to Boerne, north of San Antonio. We understand subsequent owners of the house have had similar experiences, so evidently the old woman has not given up hope of repossessing her old home.

Sam Nesmith, well-known researcher into psychic phenomena and a former member of the research staff at the Institute of Texan Cultures, says this story is a "classic case of a poltergeist." Nesmith says, "What if you were living in your home and another family moved in, too? What if you couldn't make yourself heard or seen? You'd do whatever you could to make your presence known. You'd try to drive the people away, wouldn't you?" Nesmith believes that "poltergeists can be dangerous because they are unpredictable." "All you can do is try to reason with them; to convince them they no longer need their house as much as you do."

Spirits on the South Side

On a quiet street on the south side of San Antonio, near Brooks Air Force Base, there is a house that has been the site of frequent unexplainable visits over the years, from not one, but several, other worldly presences. It isn't an unusual house . . . nothing in its outward appearance would separate it from its neighbors. But the family that has resided there has many tales to tell of unexplainable happenings at that address.

We learned of this "house of spirits" through a chance conversation with John Silva. Later, we also spoke with his sisters Maria and Sandra, all children of the widowed owner, who still resides in the house alone since the death of his beloved wife in June of 1990. The family of ten children grew up in an active household presided over by a loving mother who enjoyed her children and the various nieces and nephews and their friends who filled the house with laughter and childish pranks. Much of the time, their father, Juan, a serviceman, was away on active duty overseas, and later, after his retirement, he worked night shifts at Kelly Air Force Base, so naturally the children became very close to their mother.

John told us about many unusual and strange events that took place in the house. He said he recalled that as a child, when some of his young cousins were visiting, his mother had heard the children laughing, with obvious glee, in one of the bedrooms. She left her work in the kitchen and went to the bedroom to see what on earth was so funny. They were all in there, convulsed in laughter. She asked them what was so funny, and they told her they were laughing at "the funny stories that man sitting on the bed is telling." She saw no one. The children described him as a man wearing blue jeans and a red flannel shirt and thought it strange that Mrs. Silva did not see him, too. Many years later, John said his young son Jeddy was talking, apparently to himself . . . and when his grandmother asked him who he was talking to, he said, "to the ghost, grandmother . . . but don't worry, he's a nice ghost."

Maria Good, John's sister, spoke with us and told us one time one of her sisters, who now resides in California, was resting in one of the bedrooms. She heard children laughing and then felt someone tickling her feet. She opened her eyes to see a small blonde boy, dressed in short pants with suspenders and a striped shirt and wearing round wire rimmed glasses, standing at the foot of the bed. She thought he was a friend of her younger brother, Timmy, and told him to stop it so she could go back to sleep. He ran and opened the closet door and went inside. She closed her eyes and drifted back to sleep, and then, once again, was awakened by her feet being tickled. She told the little boy to stop once more and then called to her little brother to come tell his friend to stop. Her mother heard this and came to the room. The youngster again went into the closet. Maria and her mother opened the closet door. No one was there! The boy was never seen again!

When the Silva children were small, their dad worked a night shift. Often the children would go into the master bedroom and watch television with their mother. Sometimes they would crawl into bed with her to sleep. Once, Maria was lying in bed with her mother, when they heard a tremendous crash coming from the roof. They couldn't imagine what it was. Almost simultaneously, there was a blinding red light in the room, so bright they could not see one another, and they were literally paralyzed with fear. Maria said they couldn't even move. Then, suddenly the bright light disappeared as quickly as it had come, and they could move around again. This never happened again, although there were often loud noises heard on the roof, which sounded very much like heavy footsteps.

We also talked with Sandra, another of the Silva girls. She said she felt, as a young girl growing up there, that there was an evil presence in her bedroom. She said several times when she was about seventeen, she had heard heavy breathing at the window and thrashing about outside. Her father had gone out to investigate and found nothing. She said she had at times felt a "black . . . evil presence" in the room . . . and often, while trying to sleep, she would hear footsteps in the hall which would always stop at her door. When she ventured a peek, there would be no one there.

When they were teenagers, Sandra said the children had played with a Ouija board. Once, when they were playing with it in her room, all the curtains fell, and the Ouija marker flew off the board, while the family cat screeched and, its hair standing on end, bounded from the room!

Sandra also added that one of her brothers had distinctly heard a baby crying in one of the bedrooms one day while he was alone in the house. An investigation turned up nothing.

Several very remarkable occurrences have taken place in the house recently, since Mrs. Silva died in June of 1990. For instance, there was a ring, not an expensive piece of jewelry, but just a costume piece his mother had liked and had misplaced. After her death, John said he had found a picture he liked of his mother and had it framed. He showed it to his son Jeddy who was nineteen at the time. He was very close to his grandmother. He said, "Dad, looking at her picture I get the feeling she's trying to tell me something." That night, he dreamed about his grandmother and she told him to go over to her house and look in a "high place" and he would find the lost ring. He did go to the house the next day, and he looked on an upper shelf of her closet. Way at the back . . . was the ring!

Mrs. Silva was buried at the Fort Sam Houston National Cemetery. The services were conducted, as is customary, in a special staging area where parking is accessible. Then after the family left, the casket was removed to the designated gravesite for burial. A few days after the funeral, John's son went to the cemetery. He had never been to his grandmother's burial plot, but in all the maze of look-alike graves, he went straight to his grandmother's resting place, as if drawn there by radar. He said the night before she had appeared to him in a dream, wearing a long white gown. She told him she was fine and asked him to come and see her.

Maria told us of a strange occurrence when she first returned to visit the cemetery. She knew the section where the burial plot was located and thought she could just search until she found the exact location, never dreaming what a large area the section covered. She said the cemetery was totally deserted that day, and there was no one around to ask about the grave location. She said she looked and looked and when she could not find the grave, she said out loud . . . "Oh Mom, I just can't find you," and started to walk back to her car. She distinctly heard a voice say, "No!" She stopped suddenly, and there at her feet was her mother's marker!

When Bobby, one of the Silva boys, was home on Christmas leave from the Navy in 1990, he decided to take a nap on the living room couch. He dozed off to sleep, but was soon awakened by a whispered voice saying "Bobby . . . Bobby" . . . He thought it was his girlfriend, who was at the house for a visit. He said, "Oh, Janell, leave me alone . . . I'm trying to sleep." He dozed off again, and once more was awakened by the same voice. This time he got up to see who had called him. He looked, and found his girlfriend was outside in the yard talking to some members of the family. Then, he recalled the way his mother had always waked him up . . . with a gently whispered, "Bobby, Bobby . . . ."

Mr. Silva still lives in the house he shared so many years with his wife. John told us that recently his dad had seen a "dark shadow" pass through the bedroom, just as he was retiring for the night. The next morning he was awakened, as his wife had often done . . . by someone shaking his feet.

Maria said that prior to her death, her mother had been ill for a long while. Since she lived just across the street from her parents, Maria would go over to bathe her mother and to keep her company. Her mother knew that she was dying and often told Maria that she didn't want to die and leave her family. She asked Maria, who is the oldest daughter, to try and take care of the family. Maria feels that her mother, who was just 58 at the time of her death, still has the ability, through a loving spirit, to return to keep an eye on those she loved.

There is still no explanation for all the other "spirits" who were either seen or heard in the house for many years. Only Mrs. Silva continues to return.

The Whistling Ghost of Luckenbach

While at a recent antiques show I met a lady who owns an antique shop called Mondays Only at Boerne, north of San Antonio. Her name is Nancy Stein. Now, Nancy doesn't live in Boerne, but she grew up there and had a number of interesting Boerne ghost stories to add to our collection. She actually lives just outside the "city limits" of the famous one-store, one-house community of Luckenbach, which gained nationwide renown by the writing of the "Luckenbach, Texas" song telling about where "Willie and Wayland and the boys" loved to hang out with their old buddy, the late Hondo Crouch.

Nancy's house is just a "short piece down the road," about a half-mile from the store, off the Sisterdale Road. It's an old added-onto log settlers' house built in 1858 by the Kung brothers, Otto and Jacob. The original part of the house is a log cabin with a dog-trot and a loft. She said a stair now leads up to the loft and it is closed off by a door, which was devised to keep the downstairs warm during the winter months. For years, Nancy has been bothered by a resident ghost, and she has many fascinating stories regarding unusual disturbances to tell. She often hears a little tune being whistled by "someone or something" when she is upstairs in the loft-bedroom. The door opening to the stairwell constantly bangs open and shut. Once she tried putting a couple of sturdy chairs against the door at night to stop the noise. Next morning, the chairs were sitting, upright, clear across the room! She says the outdoor water faucet is constantly being turned on, too. There are no near neighbors, and it just isn't in the kind of community where pranksters hang out.

An old clock, "a schoolhouse type, with a pendulum" that must be wound by a key, often starts ticking, the pendulum swinging of its own volition, when she returns after a long absence. The amazing thing, she says, is that it corrects the time by itself!

Recently, Nancy was entertaining a young lady visitor. As they sat in the front room, they looked up to see a man wearing a blue shirt, "walking, all hunched over, like he was very old," striding across the front porch, from the east to the west side.

They dashed out to see who he was, and no one was there! Then, as they resettled in the front parlor, another glimpse out the window revealed the same man, this time walking back in the opposite direction, from west to east. Another look outside revealed nothing. And, strangest of all, Nancy's two schnauzer dogs had slept on the porch as the apparent intruder walked right past them. Yet, Nancy said the dogs usually were very alert and barked at anyone who came near the house!

Often pots and pans are removed from the kitchen cabinets, too. They are carefully placed in the middle of the room, on the floor.

Nancy gets disgusted with all the disturbance and has told the ghost to please "get lost," but it still persists, and she says she guesses she is glad it is a ghost and not a human being, since she lives a good distance from immediate help.

Before Nancy got involved in the antiques business she lived in Boerne, where she befriended an eccentric old lady who lived there for many years. The lady's name was Hilda Hathaway. Her house was located just behind the Country Spirits Restaurant off Main Street. It seemed that Hilda, her sister, Margaret, and her father, A. S. Hathaway, had come to Boerne from Ithaca, New York, where her father had been a professor at Cornell University. This was in the 1920s. Hilda was unmarried at the time, but while living in Boerne she met and married a man named Mr. Oltenhauser. He apparently married her for money, because he soon went off to work in the oil fields in East Texas and never came back, although she wrote begging him to return. She took her maiden name back, and that is apparently when she started getting "strange." Mr. Hathaway died, and her sister, Margaret, who suffered from tuberculosis, was placed in a sanitarium, where she eventually died.

After the death of her family, Hilda became very reclusive. Nancy said the local Boerne people made fun of her, but Nancy always liked her and felt sorry for her. Hilda had taken to wearing old men's World War I uniforms, and she also shaved her head. She always wore a strange little cloth bag, like a tobacco pouch, on a string around her neck. In it was a dried up piece of bread! Nancy never knew why Hilda did this. She collected newspapers and magazines, and never threw anything away. The house had become like a maze, a series of tunnels made up of stacks of neatly bundled papers and magazines. Bookshelves loaded with books were also everywhere in the house. Although extremely eccentric, Hilda was very intelligent and well informed, a brilliant conversationalist who could converse on any subject.

As her health began to fail, Hilda had to go to a nursing home, where she lingered on for about nine more years. Nancy continued to visit her. One of her annual "highlights" each year was to play the part of a witch during the yearly Halloween parties at the nursing home. Just after the last party she appeared at, Hilda stopped eating and refused her medication. It was as if she had just willed herself to die after that last party. She was 85 years old at the time. She apparently had no next of kin, and her funds depleted, she was given a pauper's burial, which greatly distressed Nancy. She said the only people who came to the funeral were herself, her mother, her two children, the Episcopal minister, and the funeral director. Her only flowers were in a wreath which Nancy bought.

After Hilda's death, Nancy offered to help clear out all the jumble of debris, accumulated papers, magazines, and trash, mixed with a few good antiques, that were left in the house, which had been closed up for many years. One late afternoon, after the house was locked up for the day, Nancy was standing outside the house with a man she had hired to help her clear up the rubbish. Suddenly, they heard music coming from the old piano in the house. They unlocked the house and went through the front rooms to the back room where the piano was located. As they entered the room, the music stopped. The man literally screamed in fright and ran out of the house. No amount of persuasion could get him to come back and help Nancy with the clearing out tasks.

Later on, Nancy had another unusual experience there in Boerne. One of the old Kronkosky houses had been purchased by the St. Benedictine Catholic sisters, and it had to be cleared out. Some of the items that had been part of the household had been stored in the basement for many years. Nancy and her mother, Mrs. Erna Davis, and several other people had gathered there to help price some of the items that the sisters wanted to sell. They came across an unusual urn, about eighteen inches high, which had an ornately filigreed metal base and a sort of screw-on stopper on the neck of the vessel. Nancy's mother said it looked like an urn in which the ashes of a cremated person might have been placed. Nancy pulled on the stopper, and suddenly a cloud of "thick black smoke came out of the urn, staying in a strange genie-like shape as it circled about the room, and then went right out through a closed glass window pane!" The assemblage was totally startled and completely unnerved by the experience!

Sometime later, Nancy said a lady who claimed to be a psychic visited her antique shop. She told Nancy that she was so at home among the old items in her shop because, in another life, she had lived in the Civil War era. She told Nancy that she had lost a lover in the war and had been very sad. She also told her that she had an arrow-shaped birthmark on her shoulder (she does!). The psychic told Nancy that she would have the ability to feel strange unexplained things that other people could not feel.

Well, at last report, Nancy is still being visited regularly in her Luckenbach house, and she has just come to the conclusion that maybe that psychic was right!

Castroville's Strange Spirits

Castroville is a charming old Alsatian community founded on the banks of the Medina River in 1844 by Henri Castro and his group of colonists from Alsace-Lorraine. The lovely little town is filled with darling little Alsatian cottages, each one an architectural gem. It's a pleasant place to spend an afternoon.

We were sure a community so historic would have a ghost or two, and when we started investigating, we were not disappointed! We ran into three charming ladies, longtime residents Laura McVay, Madeline Kaupt, and Jo Ann Beard, who were able to tell us a number of interesting stories about some of Castroville's ghostly residents.

We were told about a big old two-story limestone house on Gentilz Street, near the Regional Park. It seems the house, which is well over one hundred years old, was part of a large property owned by a very wealthy and prominent family. They owned considerable acreage around the house, where crops were grown, and also owned a lumber mill and a pecan orchard as well.

We were asked by our storytellers not to use the name of the original builder of the house. It seems he was a very penurious person and did not like anyone coming on his property. Now, it was pretty customary in those early days for local farmers to allow the poor people to come in and glean the fields, after the grain and corn were harvested, for any leftovers. An Indian woman came on to this particular place and the owner ran her off. He was known for his short temper, and it was said he had a hard time keeping hired help. Well, the poor lady returned again, and this time the farmer took a bullwhip to her and beat her so severely she died. We were told this occurrence is still registered in some of the old St. Louis Parish church files.

The story goes that down through the years the spirit of the dead woman keeps coming back to haunt the property, probably searching for her tormentor who, because of his wealth and influence in the community, was never brought to justice for his dastardly deed.

Various incidents would certainly indicate that hauntings have taken place in the house over the years. At one time an executive with HEB Food Company owned the house. Once, he sent his son up on the roof to adjust the television antennae. It was a warm, cloudless, sunny day. Suddenly, a huge bolt of lightening hit and knocked the young man off the roof! The soles of his shoes were burned completely off, yet he was otherwise unscathed. An arc of electricity ran from the antennae to a light pole about 700 yards away. There was no thunderstorm, no rain, and no explanation for the sudden arc of electric current.

There was a retired military couple who also once lived there, a Dr. and Mrs. Stacy. They were brilliant and well-traveled people, according to local residents, and certainly not the types to be given up to superstition. The doctor's wife was very proud of her huge collection of *National Geographic* magazines, which she kept neatly stacked and chronologically arranged in a basement area. When she would go down in the area where they were kept, sometimes she would find them tumbled about, thrown on the floor, and in complete disarray. When she would go back later, they would be back on their shelves, once more in perfect order. No explanation for these occurrences, which happened several times during the Stacy's residency, could be found.

After Dr. Stacy passed away, Mrs. Stacy remained in the house alone. She told Laura McVay, her neighbor, that she would hear the blinds going up and down in the attic window but a trip upstairs to check would reveal nothing, and the noises would stop. She would go back downstairs and the noise would start up again.

The original owner had pecan orchards. The attic was used to dry the newly harvested nuts. Mrs. Stacy said she often would hear pecans rolling around in the attic. Of course, none were there!

Once Mrs. Stacy went over to the McVays and asked Laura to come over to the house to have a glass of lemonade and "check something out." When Laura came into the kitchen, she said it was as "cold as a freezer." The hair stood up on the nape of her neck . . . she definitely felt something there. She said Mrs. Stacy felt relieved that someone else sensed the presence also. They retired to the porch for their lemonade, where the temperature was more to their liking!

Another time, Mrs. Stacy asked the McVays to come over, because she smelled the strong aroma of tobacco all over the house and wondered if they would, also. Sure enough, the place was enveloped in the pungent aroma of tobacco, although there hadn't been a pipe smoker around the house for years!

The original builder of the house had two small private cemeteries located on the property. One was a Masonic cemetery, the other was a Catholic cemetery. They remained undisturbed for years. Fairly recently, it was discovered that all the heavy gravestones in the Catholic section had been pushed over. There were no tire tracks or footprints in the area, even though it was dusty and anyone doing this would have left tracks. The official investigative report listed the occurrence as "vandalism" but nobody was really able to accept that explanation for the mysterious upheaval.

The house has changed owners several times and is now rented out. From what we hear, no one stays there very long, so the restive spirit must still be active.

Laura McVay also told us the very interesting story . . . we'll call it a "legend" . . . that has been around Castroville for a number of years. A retired World War I army captain lived with his negro house servant in a house built on the Medina River. His prize possession was a beautiful, high spirited white stallion which he often rode into town. As he grew old and feeble, the captain made his faithful servant promise that when he died the servant would kill the stallion so it would not fall into the wrong hands and be mistreated. Soon, the officer passed away and his wishes were faithfully carried out. Now, many of the people who live down near the river say that on bright moonlit nights they see the captain riding his snow white stallion along the banks of the Medina.

Seguin's Spirits at Sebastopol

East of San Antonio there is a pleasant city named Seguin. It was founded as Walnut Springs in 1838 by a member of Mathew Caldwell's Gonzales Rangers. However, they decided to change the name to Seguin a year later, in 1839. This was done to honor Juan N. Seguin, a distinguished Mexican Texan who had fought alongside Sam Houston at the Battle for Texas Independence. The illustrious Seguin later served both as a Texas senator and mayor of San Antonio.

There are many old and interesting homes and buildings in Seguin. Many were of an innovative type of construction, known as "limecrete," which was a type of concrete made from the local limestone. A physician, Dr. John E. Park, had come to Seguin from Georgia about 1847. He was very fond of natural science and chemistry. Whether he had prior knowledge or experience with concrete, or just developed a process after arriving in Seguin, is not known. Regardless of the when or how, Dr. Park learned of the qualities of aggregate wall construction, and by the time of his death in 1872 he held several patents on the production and use of concrete.

In 1854 a Colonel Joshua W. Young built a limecrete house on a rise overlooking Walnut Creek. The large home was constructed with brightly plastered walls, in a Greek Revival style. It is flat roofed, with a high-columned wrap-around porch. An innovative feature was that a water tank was placed atop the house to serve the dual purposes of storing water and cooling the house.

Colonel Young had planned to move his wife into the new house, but unfortunately she died shortly before it was completed. He then decided to give the place to his recently widowed sister, Catherine Young LeGette, who had just moved to Texas from South Carolina. This upset Young's older children, and they sued their father and his sister, their aunt, for their mother's part of the property. Mrs. LeGette finally won the rights to the house, through the intervention of the Seguin attorney John Ireland, who later became a governor of Texas.

The LeGettes lived in the house for almost twenty years. Two sons, Henry and Jesse, both left the house to serve as Confederate soldiers during the Civil War. Both returned to the house. One LeGette grandchild, Jane Yelvington McCallum, who recalled visiting the house often as a child, became the first female Secretary of State in Texas during the 1920s. In 1874, when all of her children were grown and married, Mrs. LeGette sold the house to a local merchant, Joseph Zorn, Jr.

Zorn had come to Seguin from Indiana as a youngster, with his father, Joseph Zorn, Sr., about 1850. The elder Zorn prospered, and before returning to the midwest about 1870, he had accumulated extensive property holdings in Seguin, which he left to his son. Young Zorn married Catherine "Nettie" Watkins in 1871.

The Zorns moved into the spacious house, which has been called both the Zorn House and Sebastapol, in 1874. During the last quarter of the century the house was filled with the noise and clutter common to homes with six growing children.

According to an interesting pamphlet given visitors, which was compiled by the researchers of The Texas Parks and Wildlife Department, Zorn's fortunes started to dwindle after he moved into the imposing structure. He apparently was not the astute businessman his father had been. By the 1890s his inheritance had all but disappeared. Historical archaeological investigations at the site since 1976, showing evidence of neglect and deterioration of hardware, woodwork, walls, and floors support the theory that the Zorns did not enjoy the affluence that might be expected. They attempted to project the best impression they could, since Zorn was an important and popular civic leader of Seguin.

Although not adept at managing his personal affairs, Joe Zorn was a moving force in the modernization of Seguin as it moved into the twentieth century. First, he served as an alderman and postmaster, and in 1890 he was elected mayor and held that position for twenty years. Under his leadership the community secured water, electric, and telephone services. He is best remembered for demanding an election in 1891 to create a trustee-managed free public school system. He was president of the first board of trustees. At the end of his tenure as a trustee in 1907, the district had built five new school buildings. One of Seguin's surviving limecrete structures is the Guadalupe High School built in 1850. It is the oldest continually occupied school building in the state.

After losing the mayoralty in 1910, Joe Zorn continued to serve Seguin as a civic leader until he died at Sebastopol in 1923.

Nettie Zorn passed away at the house in 1937, after having lived there for sixty-three years, but members of the family continued to reside there until the death of the youngest son, Calvert, in 1952. Threatened with demolition in 1960, the lovely old house was saved by the Seguin Conservation Society, which renovated it and operated it as a museum until 1976. In that year it was acquired by the state and today is maintained as a museum and state historical park.

One mystery concerning the house is its name, "Sebastopol." The Battle of Sebastopol, made famous in Tennyson's poem, "The Charge of the Light Brigade," took place during the Crimean War in 1854, about the time the house was built. However, that name does not appear in any documents associated with the house until the 1930s, so how it came to have the name still remains unknown.

We are indebted to Clyde Powers, a volunteer guide at Sebastopol, who shared some interesting stories about the house with us. It seems that there is a ghost or two connected with the old landmark. He told us that the story goes that once a young girl, a student at Juan Seguin School, had asked permission to be excused to go to the outhouse. When she did not return another student was sent out to check on her. It seems the girl had locked herself in the outhouse after she had seen a ghost . . . "a lady with long hair, wearing a flowing white gown." The apparition, which appeared in broad daylight, had come across the wooden bridge over Walnut Creek. The girl was so frightened she would not come out of the "necessary house."

There were three different families who reported seeing the same lady, but these appearances always happened in the dark of night. The long-haired, white-gowned figure would come from the vicinity of the old Juan Seguin School, cross over the wooden bridge which spanned the creek, and come up to Sebastopol, where she would be seen entering the downstairs east door.

Mr. Powers also told us that the son of a carpenter who worked on the house during its restoration told one of the other tour guides another ghostly story. His father had been working downstairs in the kitchen of the house. He noticed something, turned around, and saw a young boy about eight or nine years of age, with short hair, sitting in a chair watching him work. The carpenter knew he was alone, so he turned back to his work, then chanced another glance at the chair and the boy was still sitting there. He put down his tools, walked off the job, and never returned. A member of his family had to come and retrieve his tools and pick up his paycheck!

Mr. Powers said there have been no ghostly sightings lately, but who knows? They might come back at any time.

The woman in white, with the long, flowing hair, who crossed the bridge and then entered Sepastopol . . . who was she? Could she be the spirit of Catharine LeGette, who had to fight for her rights to the house? Or was it Colonel Young's wife, who died before she got to live in her lovely new home? Or was it the spirit of Mrs. Zorn, who lived there so many years? Or, could it just possibly be Seguin's version of "La Llorona," searching for her children over by Walnut Creek?

An Awareness of Things

We've a friend in San Antonio we'll call "Samantha." She is psychic, but doesn't want her real name revealed as she isn't in "the business." It's a gift she shares only with her family and close friends.

Her first unusual experience occurred when she was at work. She was a young woman working alone, and in a happy mood. Then, all of a sudden something came into her head and said to her, "Something bad is going to happen." She tried to ignore the feeling, but the inner voice kept repeating the warning to her six or seven times during the remainder of the day.

The reason for the feelings of foreboding came to her that same evening, after she had gone home. She recalled, "I stayed home by myself, took a hot bath and was getting out of the tub when I noticed that the bathroom door was slowly opening. For some reason, I hit that door with every ounce of strength I had and pushed back." She locked the door, but the doorknob kept turning and the intruder kept pushing against the door. Finally, he left, and she opened the door and then yelled to her neighbor for help. Her neighbor first called her parents, then she came over armed with a brass candlestick, entering through the back door which had been locked, but now was standing wide open. Apparently, this was where the intruder had made his exit.

It was established by investigating police that Samantha's intruder was an escaped mental patient from Chicago. While he didn't manage to reach Samantha, he went on later to attack several people in the neighborhood before he was apprehended. He attacked a nurse who was coming home from work, another lady who was coming home from an evening's engagement, and an elderly woman who was working in the alley behind her house. He had taken that woman's garden hatchet, and went after her with the makeshift weapon.

Since that time, there have been repeated psychic experiences for Samantha. The one that touched her the most was when she received the message of her own son's tragic death.

The attractive brunette repeated the story to us. "I was at the home of a friend whose father-in-law was seriously ill in another city. It was 11:30 at night as I was sitting there with my friend and I kept thinking, "He's dead." At midnight, Samantha said she looked at the clock again, and her thoughts centered on "he's been brought back to life. He's breathing!" She assumed her mental messages concerned her friend's father-in-law. It wasn't until she returned home that she found this was not the case.

When she got home, Samantha received a call concerning her son. She said, "When they found my son, he wasn't breathing. He didn't have a heartbeat, but when they wheeled him into the hospital at midnight, he started breathing again." He later succumbed. Her vigil that night had apparently been for her own son, and not the relative of her friend!

She learned later from one of her daughters that her son had appeared to the daughter as she was sitting by herself. He told her he was leaving and not to cry. He told her he loved his family. Samantha said, "My daughter went into hysterics, screaming and crying, and telling him please, not to leave us. Then another voice, which my daughter didn't recognize, came to her. It said 'we are taking him with us. Don't worry about him. He will be just fine.'"

The only communication Samantha has had with her son since that night came to her one night as she sat, crying, on the balcony of her home. "All of a sudden, I felt his hand on mine, and I heard him say, 'Don't cry, mama, I will be all right.'" Samantha said, "It was his hand, and it was his voice." While that was her last communication, Samantha has tremendous faith that her son is at peace.

Her tremendous psychic powers have extended to other areas. Once there was a house that she and her husband had considered buying. She told him she liked the house but she didn't think they should buy it because it was haunted. She had walked into two of the rooms and gotten cold chills. She was relieved when another couple purchased the house before she and her husband could make an offer.

Later, Samantha visited with the new owners of the house. She built up enough courage to inquire of them if the house was haunted. The new owner looked at her at said, "You must have ESP. Yes, the house is haunted." Later, a neighbor residing next door to the house told Samantha that she wished

Samantha and her husband could have been their new neighbors because they would have had some good times together, but she was relieved they did not buy it, because it was haunted. She told them of seeing an elderly man working in the yard and disappearing into the house on several occasions.

According to this neighbor, the house had more than one ghostly resident. She told Samantha that once the owner-parents had hired a baby-sitter. The sitter heard someone walking in the hallway. She called to the children to get back in their room. When she opened her door to look, she saw a young girl going down the stairs. After this, the children and their overnight guests would only sleep on one side of that room. They had to move the bed to accommodate their wishes!

Samantha said her husband had always been skeptical of her psychic powers, but he is beginning to realize that there are things that we must accept even though we don't understand them. She related an incident, when the couple was in another city, where her husband interviewed a man who had applied for the position of a branch office manager. "After the interview, I joined my husband and the man for cocktails. We chatted a while and then the man left. I said to my husband, 'You aren't going to hire him, are you?'" But her husband did hire the man, and he "flipped out and just took off after about six months," according to Samantha. Her feelings about the man had been right on target!

Samantha said only a couple of times had she actually seen things. She said she did this with a friend's daughter. Her friend was worried about the girl, so Samantha said, "Let me contact her." Samantha told the mother that her daughter was then sitting at a bar or counter. She was wearing a white blouse with a collar, and her hair was arranged in a pony-tail. She was drinking something and was in the company of two young men. Samantha went on to describe the men to her friend.

When her friend's daughter came home later that night, her mother had the girl call Samantha. The accurate scenario Samantha had described absolutely stunned the daughter as well as her mother!

The fact that she is especially sensitive to psychic influences is sometimes frightening to Samantha. She says she can tell the answers but can't explain the "whys." She often receives a "feeling" before she is even asked a question.

Sometimes she can just "pick up things" on people. She will ask them to write five or six things down she might tell them and then check on them and let her know if they occur within the next five or six months. She says she generalizes her predictions as going into a new business, changing jobs, or personal problems. She would never predict a divorce, but prefers to warn a friend, "Something serious may happen in your marriage in such and such a period of time."

And, in the field of predicting, Samantha boasts she has never been wrong about predicting the date of birth or the sex of her own grandchildren!

Samantha says she doesn't like antiques for some reason. They make her uneasy. While at an antiques shop one time, she said several pieces actually gave her the "willies." The clerk told her the furniture was from an estate. She began to wonder what kind of house it was, and what kind of family as the bad vibes came to her.

Now, Samantha says she has never actually seen a ghost. She refers to her "happenings" as "an awareness of things." She says, "I think what it is, and this is just my own feeling, God is all being and all things are related to Him. We don't touch it. That is our subconscious taking over and our conscious doesn't realize it. Some people have less of a division or wall between the two."

In making a prediction to a friend, Samantha says she tries to be very cautious. "I ask for God's and Jesus' protection before I do or say anything. It can be very, very frightening." Fright, in fact, sometimes causes her to turn off her feelings. When she does this, she just tries to ignore everything. She says, "You have to be able to distinguish between your own personal fears and what is happening around you." Samantha obviously realizes her psychic ability is a gift, and one that must be used wisely.

Ghost Reveals Adoption

Many years ago Rose Renee Cohen had a strange and unforgettable experience. She is convinced that a ghostly visitor came to her to let her know that she was adopted, a fact that her adoptive parents never revealed to her.

Although her family lived in San Antonio, the twenty-seven-year-old Rose was living in Tucson, Arizona at the time. One night she suddenly awoke from a deep sleep to find a man standing by her bed. "I knew it was a ghost," she said. "He just stood there and stared down at me. It seemed like ten minutes that we just looked at each other." Rose said it was strange, but she had no feeling of fright, and after the figure disappeared, she quickly went back to sleep.

About six months later, Rose returned to San Antonio to visit her mother. She had told her sister-in-law about her ghostly encounter, and so the news had already reached her mother. During a conversation soon after her arrival, Rose's mother asked her about her ghostly visitor. When Rose told her about her experience, her mother told her without any hesitation, "I know who your ghost is. Go into the bedroom and look in the bottom dresser drawer, and bring me that wooden box." Rose did as she was told, and returned carrying an old cigar box. Her mother took out a letter, and from the envelope extracted a photograph of a man. She handed the picture to Rose, and said, "This is your ghost."

The man in the picture was not very tall, and of no special significance to Rose, who wanted to know who he was. All her mother would tell her was "He was a man who loved you very much when you were a baby. He came to see you every day because he thought you were the most beautiful baby he had ever seen."

Rose asked her mother what had happened to the man. She told Rose he was killed during World War II in the Philippines.

Then, for some strange reason, Rose recalled having seen a rosary in her mother's jewelry box. She asked her mother if it had belonged to that man, and her mother said it had, indeed, belonged to the man in the photograph. Rose asked her mother if she might have it, and her mother gave her the rosary.

After they had chatted awhile, Rose's mother asked her to return the letters and the photograph to where she had found them in the dresser drawer. Because she was consumed with curiosity, Rose instead locked herself in the bathroom and began to examine the stack of letters. In so doing, she found that the man in the photo who had been the ghostly visitor was her true biological father. She said that was the first time she had had any inkling that she was adopted.

She said in reading the letters she learned that he was sent to the Philippines about a year after she was born. She also learned her biological parents had not been married and her mother had given her up for adoption.

Rose said her real parents and her adoptive parents were casual friends while the four were stationed with the Army in El Paso. They just happened to live in the same apartment complex, and that is how they became acquainted.

When Rose returned to Tucson after her San Antonio visit, she walked into the house to find the telephone ringing. Her mother was calling, in great distress. She had discovered the letters were missing from the cigar box. She wanted to know why Rose had taken them, and Rose told her she took them because she felt they were rightfully hers. Her mother urged her to never lose the letters. Still puzzled over what had happened, Rose asked her mother, "Am I adopted?" Her mother didn't want to deal with the situation and refused to answer her question. So Rose just dropped the issue.

Rose said "My adoptive mother knew it was the spirit of my real father trying to contact me, and I believed there was a reason for his appearance, too."

Nine years later Rose married David Anderson. The pair began to search for her biological mother. By that time her adoptive parents had passed away and Rose felt she could search for her natural parent without upsetting anyone.

Letters she found that her birth mother had written her adoptive mother enabled her to locate her birth certificates, both adoptive and natural, and as a consequence she learned her mother's and father's names.

After many telephone calls and letters, Rose finally found her biological mother, who was living in Michigan. She traced her father's family to where they resided on the east coast.

To Rose the whole experience was truly incredible. She is convinced if she had not been visited by the ghost of her father, she would never have found out she was adopted.

Rose said the most important thing about the whole incident was that it only made her love her adoptive parents more. After all, they had loved her, adopted her, and they wanted her. She said they thought "the sun rose and set" in her. She said she only wished they could have known how much she loved them!

Spirituality Rules

One of San Antonio's most accomplished painters is Mary Ann Hollingshead. She has won high praise for her contemporary paintings which are done with acrylic stains on a primed surface. Her work is exhibited in San Antonio at Sol Del Rio Art Gallery and also at L'Avent Musee in Paris, France.

It was only after Mary Ann had been painting over ten years that she suddenly became aware of powerful spiritual forces which seemed to influence her work. She says sometimes when a painting is at a point where it won't seemingly work out as she wants it to that she often finds it suddenly will become something far beyond what she could have done by herself. She believes that when she wants to make a painting lyric, to make it strong, to make it of the spiritual, a force beyond her own takes over. Other artists, she says, often speak of having had this same feeling, although not everyone chooses to be aware of it or to think of it.

The gifted artist terms it an element in the creative process, a pervasive feeling that something is being created far above her own limited abilities and elevates them to a higher degree.

Mary Ann says, "When this occurs, it's very exciting and reassuring and there's a feeling of confidence that the painting is working and doing what I want it to do."

Sometimes figures, which she terms "angelic forms" seem to appear in her work. Some people do not see them at all, and others say there is a definite figure in the painting. Often she is aware that people will discover a figure that she did not set out to paint.

The artist tends to paint large canvases, usually sixty-by-sixty inches, although they do vary. The largest work she has yet done is sixty inches by twenty-one feet!

Painting in the morning is the most successful time for this artist, and she loves all types of art. She has always been interested in light and color, and has wanted to create paintings reflecting something beyond what we see daily in the physical world. She says she often dreams of the colors she will use in her works.

At first Mary Ann thought she wanted to pursue a career in the advertising field. She changed her major, however, while a student at Trinity University after she had what she terms a "spiritual encounter." This experience took place one day as she walked down a hallway at the University. She came upon a little boy about six years old. He was carrying an open box, filled with the usual things that little boys collect at that age. While stopping to chat with the youngster, she said she had a distinct vision of Christ. "He came and told me he wanted me to teach." It was so vivid she changed her major to the educational field.

Mary Ann has vivid visual experiences. Once, she dreamed of a relative's death. She remembers the dream centered on a small canyon with a ravine filled with maidenhair ferns. Her relative was smiling and telling her he was all right. "The next day he was dead," she said.

She recalled when her son was two months old, she was in her kitchen alone on Thanksgiving morning. As she went about preparing the family dinner, she had the distinct feeling that her grandmother, who had been dead ten years, and her uncle, who had been gone fourteen years, were in the kitchen with her. They had come to see the baby son who had been born in September. Although she "felt" more than she "saw," she said she did see their full forms, though not as distinctly as they would have been in life. They appeared as soft, hazy figures, she explained.

Another profound experience for the artist came two years ago, when two things made her conscious that a deceased aunt was trying to tell her something. On a Saturday morning she had a sudden urge to clean a certain bureau drawer that she had not touched in twenty-five years. At the bottom of the drawer was a yellow envelope with a poem in it her aunt had written to her mother at Mary Ann's birth. She said she felt very close to her aunt that day.

Another time, the family was seated around the dining room table where they had been talking about that same aunt. Suddenly, an apple, which had been in a large bowl on the center of the table for several hours just up and rolled out on the table. Mary Ann said the family all laughed about the incident. They felt sure their aunt had given the apple a nudge!

CHAPTER 4

Military Posts Have Military Ghosts

GHOSTLY PRANKS FROM AMONG THE RANKS
Docia Williams

Around and about old Fort Sam Post
'Tis said, there are some lively ghosts.
"Black Jack" Pershing is said to still roam
O'er the grand old house he used to call home.
While down the street, on old Staff Post
At Number One, there once was a ghost.
And at Service Club Two, for enlisted ranks,
"Harvey," the ghost, used to pull pranks.
His footsteps would echo on the upstairs floors,
And he often would open the windows and doors.
Down at Ft.Clark, there's a ghost "cook" and a "cat."
Ever heard a stranger story than that?

"Harvey"... the Harlequin Ghost

The U.S. Army arrived in San Antonio in 1845. Known as Fort Sam Houston, the military installation has been in its present location since 1876. There are several spirits that have been known to hang around the post. Perhaps the most interesting of the stories is the one related to us by John Manguso, curator of the Ft. Sam Houston Museum. He shared some fascinating information with us from the museum files about "Harvey," who, it was said, was a well-known resident spirit that used to call Service Club Number Two his "home away from home" for a number of years.

It seems that doors used to slam and windows would open at odd times, and footsteps would echo in empty rooms. Sometimes it was reported that a typewriter carriage would travel back and forth as if guided by unseen hands. Music used to be heard coming from the ceiling. The people who worked around the club started calling the mischievous interloper "Harvey."

Harvey was more or less taken for granted, so commonplace were the incidents of his mischief-making. Time and again the club would be locked up and secured for the night, and the manager at the time, Phyllis Boyes, who was there in 1967-68, said when she would go home for the evening, satisfied that all was well at the club, she would be summoned by the Military Police, who discovered unlocked doors and windows at the club when they made their rounds. No matter the hour, she would have to return to the empty club and lock up again. This happened a number of times and must have been pretty maddening.

Heavy footsteps would be heard on the second floor of the club, but when searchers looked over the area, they could never find a thing. Witnesses also reported that they often heard the characteristic sounds made by a ping-pong ball as it would be batted back and forth across a table tennis net... but there would be no one in the room... unless the players were unseen spirits, that is.

Army First Sergeant Louis Milligan also made mention of Harvey's existence in the article that Mr. Manguso shared with us. He described how, one evening, when everything was locked and all personnel were departing, music, which seemed to come from the ceiling and sounded like it was made by a flute, was heard. He went upstairs to investigate and the music stopped. Upon his return downstairs, it started up again.

Shortly after the music incident, a typewriter went into action unaided by human hands. A couple of soldiers were in the room at the time, but both had their backs to the machine. They suddenly heard the carriage slide across the typewriter so hard the little bell at the end of the line rang. Yet another person reported hearing someone (it must have been Harvey!) clear his throat. The lady was putting some food into the club's refrigerator when she distinctly heard someone "Harrumph" right behind her. She turned, and no one was there.

Now, just who was Harvey . . . and why did he hang around the service club? No one knows for sure, but a commonly accepted theory was that he was the unsettled spirit of a young man who had committed suicide at the club. Only the fact of the young man's violent death . . . and not the "why" of it, is known. We were told the spirit of Harvey had apparently been gone from the club for some time.

And then . . . only recently, we became acquainted with Florence Buntin, who is the charming Promotions-House Manager for the popular Harlequin Dinner Theatre, which now makes its headquarters in the former service club. We told her we knew the story of Harvey's former occupancy at the club, and she said, "You know, we still have a ghost at the theatre." She referred us to Bruce Shirky, who is the artistic director of the playhouse. Mr. Shirky verified the fact there was, indeed, a ghost at the theatre, and he had not only heard it, but had actually seen the apparition!

Shirky said, about four years ago, he had come to the building to do some work one evening. He had just started to go upstairs, when suddenly he heard footsteps up above him. Looking up the stairs, he caught a glimpse of a figure passing by in the hallway above him. He rushed up the stairs and searched the entire floor . . . but found nothing . . . not a trace! He first thought maybe the janitor had been there, but how could he have just disappeared? He hurried downstairs, and found the janitor at work in the dish-washing room. When he was questioned, he said he had not been upstairs at all! Shirky says he is positive he saw the figure upstairs!

He also said that the staff at the Harlequin all feel a "presence" from time to time. He also said windows go up and down, and doors open and close, with no plausible reason. "And things seem to get moved around." He said the presence is not unpleasant, but sometimes the building does feel a little "eerie" to him.

Shirky said he knows that two deaths occurred on the premises. A young soldier (could it have been Harvey?) is said to have hanged himself in the men's room, and a young boy drowned in the swimming pool that was once located back of the building when it was a service club. Whether the current resident ghost is Harvey, or another restive spirit that has moved in on his former territory, we are not prepared to say . . . .

Are You There, General Pershing?

We were recently privileged to have a brief visit with Mrs. Dorothy Stotser, wife of Lt. General George R. Stotser, Commander of the Fifth Army at Fort Sam Houston. She graciously showed us through the first floor rooms of the spacious Commander's home on Staff Post Road known as the Pershing House. The beautiful old limestone house was designed by Alfred Giles, a famous architect at the time. Constructed in 1881, the house is the largest of a line of houses situated along the tree-lined boulevard. Named for one of its most famous residents, General of the Armies John J. "Black Jack" Pershing, who lived there from February to May of 1917, it has long been the home of the ranking general on the post.

Mrs. Stotser gave credence to stories we had heard rumored, but had not been able to substantiate, that the historic landmark is haunted. She said she believes the ghost is "friendly," and therefore no real bother, but a "very interesting topic of conversation." She definitely believes the ghost is that

of General Pershing. At the time he resided in the house he had been newly and tragically bereft of his wife and three of his four small children. They had perished in a fire in the Pershing quarters at the Presidio of San Francisco, while General Pershing was struggling to keep things in line along the Texas border. This was in 1916, during the Pancho Villa uprisings. Stunned by his loss, a lonely and depressed widower, he was soon posted to Fort Sam Houston where he took up residence in the Commander's house. He did not remain long at Fort Sam Houston, because in May of 1917 he was called to command the Expeditionary Forces in Europe during World War I.

Mrs. Stotser said the main evidences of something unusual during her residency in the house has been the frequent flushing of the commodes in the middle of the night, or the doorbell would ring, and no one would be there. She said she feels that "General Pershing gets bored, especially at night, and wakes up the occupants for company." She added that there had been no recent occurrences.

Our conclusions are that maybe General Pershing's spirit returns to the house where he was so grief-stricken after the loss of his wife and children and he can't rest because he was unhappy in the house. Or, another possibility . . . feeling honored that the Commander's House has been named for him, maybe he just wants to check up on the general welfare of the house and its occupants, who, just as he did, are still faithfully serving their country.

The Ghost of Quarters Number One

The beautiful tree-shaded street, known as Staff Post Road on Fort Sam Houston, is a quiet haven for those who reside there, in the lovely old limestone houses built in 1881.

Many famous army officers have resided in these houses, and the area provides a restful atmosphere for the officers and their families privileged to make their homes on that part of the post. However, Number One, which is at the very beginning of the road, adjacent to Grayson Avenue, was once haunted. John Manguso, the curator at the Fort Sam Houston Museum, told us that museum visitors have said that the quarters were once occupied by an officer who had access to government funds, as he was one of the finance officers. He evidently dipped into the coffers, and with his ill-gotten gains was able to build up a nestegg to be used for his retirement. Unfortunately for him, he was caught, red-handed. Rather than "face the music," he committed suicide.

Following this, several residents of Quarters Number One reported that toilets would flush when no one was around, and footsteps would be heard, and a presence felt. One woman felt something sit down on the bed next to her, but of course, no one was there!

We were discussing some of the ghost stories we had collected at a recent gathering of friends, and Colonel George Rodgers, USA, Retired, volunteered that he have lived in Number One in 1976 and 1977, and that the house was indeed haunted at that time. He said his wife first heard the heavy footsteps walking the upstairs hallways, and later, he also heard them on numerous evenings. He said his wife also heard something walking up the stairs as well. He said he was never particularly disturbed, but his wife found the presence of a night-walking spirit very unnerving.

It is our understanding that the spirit has not been active for several years. It is hoped that he has finally settled into a peaceful existence in his eternal resting place.

Chapter 4

Pedro Struts Again

Pedro was special! The feathered "personality," a colorful Bantam rooster, was one of the most popular residents of the Fort Sam Houston Quadrangle for many years. Hatched in April of 1953, he soon became "king of the roost," and was allowed full run of the place. No office, including that of the commanding general, was considered to be off-limits to Pedro. It was said he crowed right along with reveille most every morning!

The story as related to us by a longtime San Antonio resident, John Tolleson, says that in the early 1960s when a new commanding general arrived on the post, he swept into his new office only to find Pedro perched on the desk. Pedro had just finished doing what roosters do sometimes on the desk. The general, not realizing the prominence and privilege accorded the colorful bird, called for a sergeant to come remove the culprit from his office. In fact, it is said the sarge was ordered to "execute this creature . . . wring its neck . . . and then I'd like to have him served up for supper tonight." It seems the sergeant complied, but only up to a point. The general is said to have dined on (commissary) chicken and dumplings that night. The popular Pedro was securely sequestered away from the Quadrangle and the eyes of the new general for the length of his tenure at Fort Sam Houston. Word soon got around that Pedro was no more.

When the general was transferred to another post, Pedro was returned to his rightful place at the Quadrangle. Many people, having believed him long since dead, thought they were seeing a chicken ghost when Pedro reappeared. However, Pedro lived out his happy and freedom-filled life in friendly security until he died of natural causes in June of 1966 at the age of thirteen years and two months. He was honored with a special burial plot and grave marker just behind the clock tower in the center of the Quadrangle.

Now, many old-timers who "knew" Pedro during his "salad days" swear that when the Fifth Army Band lines up in parade formation to perform at a special ceremony in the old Quadrangle, they have seen the ghost of the cocky little rooster "marching like a little drum major" right up in front of the army band!

The Cook and the Cat

During a recent weekend visit with friends at Fort Clark Springs, we met the genial curator of the Old Fort Clark Guard House Museum, Mr. Don Swanson. A tour of the museum revealed many interesting facts about the historic fort, founded by the U.S. Army on June 20, 1852. Mr. Swanson was kind enough to share a good ghost story taken from the museum's archives, about one of the officer's quarters on Colony Row. Most of the limestone quarters, built around 1874, have been restored and are now the homes of retired couples who live on the fort property which has been "recycled" into a beautiful resort area. Number One, a one-story dwelling at the end of the row is unoccupied, boarded up, and has a desolate, lonely, out-of-place look among its beautifully restored neighbors. Perhaps there's a good reason why!

Mr. Swanson told us the author Kenneth Wiggins Porter wrote the following story after he interviewed Mrs. Lucius Holbrook, widow of General Lucius R. Holbrook, in 1955. Mrs. Holbrook said the story had been related to her by General Howard R. Laubach, a former resident of the fort.

"General Laubach reported to Fort Clark in June 1894 as a recent graduate of the Military Academy at West Point. As a very junior second lieutenant, Laubach was assigned Company B, 23rd Infantry under the command of Colonel J. J. Coppinger, who also commanded the post at Fort Clark at that time.

"Lt. Lauback was intending to be married in the very near future, so at the time of reporting he made an inquiry to the commanding officer on the availability of married officer's quarters. The C.O. stated the only quarters available was a little square one-story building at one end of the Officers' Row. He also emphasized the reason that the building was vacant was due to general belief at the post that it was haunted. As a background for this belief the commanding officer stated that a colonel (probably H. M. Lazelle) who formerly commanded the post, had lived in that house. He had a female colored cook who was always accompanied by a big black cat. The colonel was known to be a heavy drinker, and when inebriated, he sometimes beat the cook. Eventually, after one such beating, the cook died. After that, people in the living room of the little house reported they would hear footsteps on the ceiling, which would come down the wall and go halfway across the room, and then suddenly stop. People then began to see the cook and her cat. Finally, no one could be found who was willing to live in the quarters. Once, a colored servant, who was lodged there overnight without being told of the house's reputation, was found sitting on the porch the next morning. He had heard the footsteps and made a fast retreat, deciding to leave the house to the cook and the cat.

"Lt. Laubach was concerned over the effect such a visitation might have on his future bride. The commanding officer was concerned also and he repeated all the stories he had previously been told, with some new ones added, in support of his belief that the bride would not wish to live there. However, the brave young lieutenant, not wishing to lose the only opportunity for married officers' quarters, decided to move into the little house.

"Now, Laubach had two dogs. One was rather valuable. For some time neither he nor the dogs heard or saw anything out of the ordinary. Then, one night at eleven p.m., as the lieutenant was getting ready to inspect the guard as Officer of the Day, he heard footsteps walking across the ceiling, which moved down the wall and came towards him to the middle of the floor. His dogs were so terror-stricken that they dashed through the screen window and screen porch. The most valuable dog completely lost his senses and had to be tied up. Eventually he had to be destroyed. The other dog could never be coaxed into the house again.

"Later, after Lt. Laubach married and brought his young wife to live in Quarters Number One, he was relieved that she never heard anything at all alarming. Whether her presence laid the ghost to rest for good, or not, the general did not know. At any rate, after leaving Fort Clark he never heard anything further about the haunted house he had once occupied."

The present long vacancy . . . no buyers . . . no takers . . . makes us wonder if maybe the cook and the cat have returned to Colony Row!

AND SO IN CLOSING
Docia Williams

There are ghosts that are legend . . . and ghosts that are real,
With footsteps you hear, and cold spots you feel . . . .
They come out each night, when the bright sun goes down,
And watchfully guard this sleeping old town.
San Antonio has many . . . we've named but a few,
Some, you may question, but most all are true!

SOURCES

Newspapers:
The Houston Chronicle
Oct. 25, 1987
The San Antonio Light
Oct. 28, 1990; Feb. 16, 1991
The San Antonio Express News
March, 1890; Feb. 5, 1894; Aug. 23, 1897; Feb. 9, 1965;
Feb. 12, 1965; Feb. 15, 1965; Feb. 17, 1965; Feb. 23,
1965;March 5, 1965; March 8, 1965; June 23, 1965; Aug.
6, 1965; Sept. 4, 1965; May 9, 1971; Oct. 31, 1974; Nov.
14, 1980; Sept. 25, 1981; Aug. 1, 1982; Oct. 1, l982; Oct.
31, 1984; Nov. 2, 1988; Oct. 19, 1989; Aug. 12, 1990.

Magazines and Periodicals:
San Antonio Express News Magazine Section
Oct. 28, 1984; Oct. 31, 1984; Nov. 2, 1988; Nov. 26, 1989
Leon Springs Chronicle, Vol. 1, No. 8
June 1982
Ye Kendall Inn Gazette
San Antonio Conservation Society News
May, June 1992
Texas Highways Magazine
October 1983
San Antonio Monthly Magazine
October 1981
Texas Monthly Magazine
October 1978

Pamphlets:
"A History of San Antonio's Menger Hotel" published by
National Trust for Historic Preservation
"The Gunter Hotel" by Mary Ann Noonan Guerra
"Sebastopol State Historical Park" published by Texas
Parks and Wildlife Department

Stories:
Thesis. "Hope Farm, A Century of Change," Tim Swan, December 11, 1973
"A Ghost Story from Fort Clark" by Kenneth Wiggins Porter, from archives of Fort Clark Guard House Museum

Books
Legendary Ladies of Texas published by Texas Folklore Society XLIII in cooperation with the Texas Foundation for Woman's Resources
Mysterious San Antonio by David Bowser published by the writer

Personal Interviews
We wish to especially thank the following individuals who shared information with us in the form of personal and telephone interviews:
Mr. Ken Alley, Leon Valley Historical Society
the late Mike Anderson
Rose Renee Anderson
Jo Ann Andrews, owner, Victoria's Black Swan Inn
Christina Autrey
Audrey Baros
Jo Ann Beard, historian, Castroville
Laura Beckley
David Bowser, author, *Mysterious San Antonio*
Florence Buntin, Promotions-House Manager, Harlequin Dinner Theatre
Frank Castillon, Chief Investigator, Office of Bexar County Medical Examiner, and homicide detective, retired, San Antonio Police Department
Julia Cauthorn, owner, Sartor House, King William Historic District
Brian Cobb, Director, Alamo Street Theatre
Jackie Contreras, formerly executive staff, Sheraton Gunter Hotel

Cathy Cummins, Enrichment Director, San Antonio Academy

Seymour Dreyfus, owner, Hope Farm

Mary Diaz Garcia

Betty Gatlin, owner, Lavender House

Lillian Gonzales

Maria Silva Good

Ilse Griffith, longtime resident, King William Historic District

Denice Hardy, former manager, Settlement Inn

Marjorie Hardy, President, Daughters of the Republic of Texas

Kathy Hendrix

Mary Ann Hollingshead

John Igo, lecturer, professor, San Antonio College

Madeline Kaupt, historian, Castroville

Rosamond Lane

Helen Lampkin, the *San Antonio Express News*

Bill and Marcie Larsen, owners, the Alamo Street Restaurant

Vivis Lemmons, Institute of Texan Cultures

Charles Long, Curator Emeritus, The Alamo

Henry Mahler, former resident, Mahler House

John Manguso, curator, Fort Sam Houston Museum

Reba Marshall

Sue Martin, owner, Country Spirit Restaurant, Boerne

Lynne McClanahan

Nicki Frances McDaniel, writer, San Antonio *Express News*

David McDonald, Texas Parks and Wildlife Department

Laura McVay, historian, Castroville

Ingeborg Mehren, former owner, the Mehren House

Sam Nesmith, military historian, psychic consultant

Barbara Hunt Niemann, homicide detective, retired, San Antonio Police Department

The late Henry Nussbaum, executive staff, Sheraton Gunter Hotel

Kendall County Judge Garland Perry

Fred Plank

Sources

Clyde Power, volunteer docent, Sebastapol House, Seguin
Ramon Ramos
Peggy Redman
Frieda Reed
Jessie Rico, custodian, The Spanish Governor's Palace
Colonel George Rodgers, US Army, Retired
Rosalie Ross
Toni Rossignol, docent, Institute of Texan Cultures
Jerry Salazar, *San Antonio Express News*
Jesse Sanchez
Julia Scheibe
Milton Schelper
Vicki Schleyer, owner, Ye Kendall Inn
Bruce Shirky, Artistic Director, Harlequin Dinner Theatre
John Silva
Jackie Sparks, choreographer, San Antonio Little Theatre
Steven Spence, Settlement Inn
Nancy Stein, owner, Mondays Only Antiques Shop, Boerne
Mrs. George R. Stotser
Theda Sueltenfuss
Don Swanson, curator, Old Fort Clark Guard House
    Museum
John Tolleson, San Antonio City Guide and Historian
Rich Villarreal, caretaker, Ye Kendall Inn
William Ward, Institute of Texan Cultures
Judy Wasson
Chester Webb, former resident, Wolfson Manor
Olive White
Sidney Yarbrough, San Antonio Conservation Society

All photos taken by authors with exception of the Gunter Hotel, which is used with permission of the hotel executive staff.

Index

Regional Books From Wordware

100 Days in Texas: The Alamo Letters

A Cowboy of the Pecos

A Treasury of Texas Trivia

Alamo Movies

At Least 1836 Things You Ought to Know About Texas but Probably Don't

Black Warrior Chiefs: The History of the Seminole Negro Indian Scouts

Civil War Recollections of James Lemuel Clark and the Great Hanging at Gainesville, Texas in October 1862

Cow Pasture Pool: Golf on the Muni-Tour

Cripple Creek Bonanza

Daughter of Fortune: The Bettie Brown Story

Defense of a Legend: Crockett and the de la Peña Diary

Don't Throw Feathers at Chickens: A Collection of Texas Political Humor

Eight Bright Candles: Courageous Women of Mexico

Etta Place: Her Life and Times with Butch Cassidy and the Sundance Kid

Exiled: The Tigua Indians of Ysleta del Sur

Exploring Dallas with Children: A Guide for Family Activities

Exploring the Alamo Legends

Eyewitness to the Alamo

From an Outhouse to the White House: A Primer on Arkansas and Tennessee Words and Ways

The Funny Side of Texas

Ghosts Along the Texas Coast

The Great Texas Airship Mystery

Henry Ossian Flipper: West Point's First Black Graduate

Horses and Horse Sense: The Practical Science of Horse Husbandry

How the Cimarron River Got Its Name and Other Stories About Coffee

The Last Great Days of Radio

Letters Home: A Soldier's Legacy

More Wild Camp Tales

Noble Brutes: Camels on the American Frontier

Outlaws in Petticoats and Other Notorious Texas Women

Phantoms of the Plains: Tales of West Texas Ghosts

Rainy Days in Texas Funbook

Red River Women

Santa Fe Trail

Slitherin' 'Round Texas: A Field Guide for People Who Don't Like Snakes

Spirits of San Antonio and South Texas

Star Film Ranch: Texas' First Picture Show

Tales of the Guadalupe Mountains

Texas Highway Humor

Texas Politics in My Rearview Mirror

Texas Tales Your Teacher Never Told You

Texas Wit and Wisdom

That Cat Won't Flush

That Old Overland Stagecoaching

This Dog'll Hunt

To The Tyrants Never Yield: A Texas Civil War Sampler

Tragedy at Taos: The Revolt of 1847

A Trail Rider's Guide to Texas

Unsolved Texas Mysteries

Western Horse Tales

Wild Camp Tales